Mercy Me

Mercy Me

A Novel

Margaret A. Graham

Fleming H. Revell
A Division of Baker Book House Co
Grand Rapids, Michigan 49516

Published by Fleming H. Revell
a division of Baker Book House Company
P.O. Box 6287, Grand Rapids, MI 49516-6287
www.bakerbooks.com

Printed in the United States of America

Library of Congress Cataloging-in-Publication Data
Graham, Margaret, 1924–
    Mercy me : a novel / Margaret A. Graham.
        p.   cm.
    ISBN 0-8007-5873-0 (pbk.)
    1. Women—Fiction. 2. Church membership—Fiction. 3. City and
town life—Fiction. I. Title.
PS3557.R2157M47 2003
813′.54—dc21   2002154758

Scripture is taken from the King James Version of the Bible.

For Bunny Dagley
who loves all God's creatures, great and small,
especially Paso Fino horses

And God, who studies each commonplace soul,
Out of commonplace things makes His beautiful whole.

Sarah Chauncet Woolsey
(Susan Coolidge, pen name)

1

❧

Dear Beatrice,

You have not wrote in a long time. Are you all right? Let me know if you are sick.

As for me, my aches and pains come from having too many birthdays. Only good thing about birthdays is getting old enough to get that Social Security check. But before I leave the planet, I got a few things to let you in on.

For one thing, I'm here to tell you that there is not one word of truth in that old saying "There's no fool like an old fool." Make no mistake, there's lots of competition out there, fools young and old with no more smarts than that state house crowd. I got a long way to go to be the fool them baby boomers is, right? To keep the playing field fair (Ha! Ha!) I am not taking any of them mind-enhancing herbs them women in the Willing Workers Sunday school class swear by.

Beatrice, you might know the Willing Workers is at it again. This time they're in a swivet to run off the new music director. As for me, I'm sitting tight. Mercy me, the fellow is not dry behind the ears.

I got the garden plowed. Elijah'll come grub it up so I can start planting come Good Friday.

Your friend,

Esmeralda

It took me a while to get that letter mailed. You'd think that since Bud died I would've had plenty of time, but first one thing and another came up, and before I knew it, my day was gone. Went to the hardware store and bless Patty if the boy Elmer hired part-time didn't try to sell me last year's seed corn. I marched right back in the office and told Elmer to get that sack of corn off the floor before some unsuspecting customer bought it and it don't half come up.

Well, to get back to Beatrice, I worried about her up there in Mason County with nobody to look after her. Like me, she had no family to speak of, one cousin out West, maybe in Idaho. She is old as me by a few months, but she still had not got the sense God promised a billy goat. When the mill closed here in Live Oaks, the only place she could find a job was at a convenience store up on the interstate at Piney Woods Crossroads. I didn't worry about the locals holding up the store—the moonshine business is still going strong in Mason County—but people coming off the interstate are from all over and be not above pulling a gun on somebody. I knew that if ever that place was robbed, nervous as she was, she'd like as not drop dead before they could get off a shot.

Well, I finally got the letter mailed, and as soon as Beatrice got it, she called me up. She started in right away, telling me she was not sick.

"My dreaded disease has not come back on me yet. I've got no more lumps, but that don't mean I'll live long enough to pay all these here medical bills."

"The Lord will provide," I told her, but she wasn't listening. She was talking fast and cramming her words together to get as much said as she could without running up a big phone bill. That's the way she always starts out, rapid as machine-gun fire, but usually she winds down and yackety-yacks to her heart's content.

She was telling me, "The reason I haven't wrote much lately is because I can't think of nothing to write about. All I do is work all day, walk home of an evening, eat a TV supper, wash my underwear, and read my devotional. Then I make sure all the doors and winders is locked and check to make sure my will is safe under the mattress. Then I go to bed."

By then she had used up all she had to say, but her lonesome self wouldn't allow her to say good-bye.

"Esmeralda," she said, "you're right about them baby boomers. Yesterday one of them dropped a penny on the floor, and he made not a move to pick it up. That's the way they are—give 'em pennies in change and they leave 'em on the counter. Ain't it in the Bible about a penny saved is a penny earned? Well, like as not, they don't read the Bible. I don't call nobody a fool, but one of them comes in here and feeds quarters to the video machine till he has not got a quarter left."

I laughed a little to let her know I was still listening, but I didn't say anything—didn't want to encourage her to stay on the line. She hung on anyway, trying to think of something more to say. Her pauses are like when the washing machine stops between cycles then starts up again.

"I sure miss Tom," she whined. "I'd like to have me another companion, but I am sure not looking for one. Nobody can take Tom's place."

I was about to say something, but she changed the subject. "What's that music director's name?" she asked. "I sure miss Apostolic Bible Church and the Willing Workers. I guess Clara is still head of the W.W.s because she has not died yet."

I finally decided that if Beatrice was going to talk all night, I might as well butt in and say a few things myself. "Before you pass judgment on that fool who feeds the video machine, there's Willing Workers that buys all kinds of magazines they don't read, hoping they'll win the sweepstakes. They say it's not gambling because they get something for their money. Besides, they say, if they win the sweepstakes, they'll give some of the money to Apostolic Bible Church and a lot of it to missions. I'll not say what I think, but Splurgeon says, 'He who gambles picks his own pocket.' That's the truth if ever I heard it."

I didn't give her a chance to ramble off again, because I needed to jerk a knot in her about eating TV dinners.

"And what do you mean eating TV dinners?" I said. "You're a good cook even if you are a rich cook. All that butter and cream is good tasting and a lot better for you than food froze for years that tastes like wallpaper paste."

"They ain't so bad, Esmeralda. Why should I cook up a lot of stuff when there's only me to eat it? I use to cook chicken for Tom."

"Well, Beatrice, that brings me to something else. I've been telling you for some time that you need to get out more and meet people. Tom was as good a friend as a four-legged critter can be, even though he took off now and then to go courting. But what you need is a two-legged, talking friend. Better yet, a man friend."

I thought she would go ballistic, but to her, the idea of having a man friend was so out of the question that it didn't bother her. "Oh, I'm too old for that," she said. "Marriage ain't for me."

"You don't have to marry him! It's just you need a friend to go out to eat with once in a while. As for marriage, you would've been married long ago if it wasn't for that hang-up you've got. When you were young and ripe, you dumped every boy that showed you favor because they didn't come up to your standards. Whatever you meant by that, I'll never know. With men so scarce in Live Oaks, a girl had to take what she could get. Of course, I got the cream of the crop, but every fellow that asked you for a date you compared him to your sweet patootie, Percy Poteat. After the way he made fun of you all through school, I don't see how you could have ever given him the time of day. Mercy me, he used to tell you you were ugly and that your mama dressed you funny! Of course, like me, you weren't so favored in the looks department, and it was true your mama had only one pattern—one week a blue jumper and the next week a brown one. And them hair bows were way too big. But when your mama curled your hair, you looked like a store-bought doll."

"That was a long time ago, Esmeralda. And if beauty is a curse, I was mighty blessed."

She had said that so many times it wasn't funny anymore. "Beatrice, there was one time when you were a real good looker. Do you remember? It was after we quit school to go to work in the variety store. The manager assigned you to the candy counter, and you really filled out then. That's when all the boys tried to get you to go steady. That's when those flat-chested, green-with-envy Neely girls started razzing you about your red hair. Jealous, that's all. They were just plain jealous and stayed green with envy until you turned against Hershey kisses and slimmed down again. And as long as you eat them TV dinners, you will keep on being skinny as a rail."

I could hear her loud sigh over the phone. "I guess I am right bony in parts."

"You are not bony! You could just use a little more meat on you is all. Why, Clara Wolf would give her upper plate to have your figure. There ought to be some nice wifeless man at church or one that comes in the station you could go out with. I bet you don't even cast an eye to see."

"I'm way too busy to notice anybody comes in that place."

Busy, my eye! All her life, Beatrice had been shy. At a party, you might as well have pasted her on the wall and called her "Miss Wallflower." Beatrice was not at ease in her own skin, and there was no reason for that. Even at her age, she still had eye appeal, and if she would put her mind to it, I knew she could be a knockout. I racked my brain trying to think of something that would improve her appearance.

"Beatrice, why don't you color your hair? Get yourself a bottle of hair dye and get rid of that faded look you got now. You don't need to worry about it being a sin to put the color back the way God made you in the first place."

"We better hang, Esmeralda, or I won't be able to pay the bill. But wait, now—you were going to tell me the name of that music director."

"His name? It's Boris Krantz, and that's another thing them women at church can't abide. Nobody around here has got a name like that, and you know if Clara can't climb down your family tree to the bare roots, you don't get no clean bill of health. He's a right nice-looking boy, and if he gets to stay here long enough, chances are he'll marry one of our girls. I say new blood is a good thing. All this inbreeding such as we have got here in Live Oaks is not good for the community. Now you hang up the phone and go cook yourself some red meat."

13

She hung up, and I went in the kitchen to fry some potatoes. I thought that for somebody with mile-high medical bills, she sure ought to hold down on long-distance calls. Long distance is many a woman's fast track to the poorhouse.

I told myself I'd try to remember to call her the next time. I wondered if she'd take me up on dyeing her hair.

2

I had a lot to do the following week. Elijah came and grubbed up the garden. I tell you, that old mule of his looked like she wouldn't last long, but, of course, Maude had always looked thataway. Coming down the street, she would lean to one side and the wagon would lean to the other. They creaked along at a snail's pace, and Elijah just sat there letting Maude take the lead. If truth be told, I thought Elijah might not outlast Maude. Sometimes he was so stove up he could hardly climb down from the wagon.

I remember a time when he was working for Clara, when his slow pace provoked her so much she took the hoe out of his hands and showed him how to speed up. Elijah took off his cap, wiped his brow, and politely told her, "Miz Clara, you do's it a minute or two; I do's it from sunup to sundown."

That put the quietus on her, and she marched right back in the house. I laugh every time I think about that.

Clara is one of those women who wants to run things. The week Elijah grubbed my garden, she got the notion that we needed to put down carpet in the Willing Workers classroom and asked every member to bring fifty cents a week until we got the money to pay for it. I couldn't figure what she had against vinyl. I, for one, thought it was just fine, a lot cleaner than carpet. I thought what money we had ought to go to missions, but when I said that, you won't believe what she said back. With her mouth twisted in a know-it-all knot, she told me, "You sound like Judas."

I thought I was going to come out of my chair, and I probably would have if Thelma had not grabbed my arm.

With them tight lips, Clara proceeded to explain. "It's told us in the gospel that when Mary poured perfume on Jesus, Judas asked, 'Why wasn't that ointment sold and the money given to the poor?'"

Nobody in the room got the connection, so Thelma spoke up. "What's that got to do with this carpet?"

To give answer, Clara's voice rose, and she let go the twist-lip mode. "It means that there is a time when we're supposed to lavish our attention on the Lord by spending a little money to make his house beautiful. I am sure Solomon had a carpet on the floor of that temple he built for the Lord. We're not supposed to be so practical when it comes to worshiping God."

I couldn't help myself; it popped right in my head what Mr. Splurgeon said about temples. "It is easier to build temples than to be one," I told them.

Clara looked about to pop her cork. "That has nothing to do with this," she spluttered.

Thelma is just about the only one in the group who has the backbone to stand up to Clara. "Well, Clara," she said, "all of this you're saying about our floor and Solomon's temple seems far-fetched. I don't think we're ready to plunk out a lot of money for a carpet, are we ladies?"

They all agreed, except Mabel Elmwood, who always goes for keeping up appearances.

Well, I give Clara this. She knows when to quit. "All right, then," she said, "we'll just lay the matter on the table."

Of course, that meant she wasn't giving up, but for the time being she would change the subject. She cleared her pipes and put on a long face. "We have got to be praying about this situation in the music department," she informed us, as if prayer were really what she had in mind. "All the teenagers are going hog wild over Boris Krantz, and we have got to put a stop to that. Why, I heard—Well, never mind," she said, knowing every last one of us wanted to know what she'd heard. She shook her head and put on that gloom-and-doom look, as if it were too grave a matter to reveal in only a few minutes. That's the way she is—likes to hold you in suspense while she makes up as much as she can to add to whatever it is she's going to tell.

"We'll have the lesson now," she said and turned the class over to Thelma.

Thelma had lived in Chicago and years back went to a Bible institute. Said she started out to be a missionary but wound up at Live Oaks, where she felt she was most needed. If you ask me, she was still looking for a husband and this was the end of the line. After gleaning through the slim pickings here, she gave up and settled in instead of moving on.

Thelma was a fair to middlin' teacher, but we all studied the quarterly and knew what she was going to say before she said it. I did listen to make sure she didn't slip up and bring in some false doctrine. To her credit, though, she was always there and never late. That goes along with being a Yankee.

The bell rang.

Well, I was glad class was over. It was stuffy in there, and I wanted to get in line for the bathroom. My bladder does not get the good mileage it used to.

Monday I got a letter from Beatrice, which reminded me that I had planned to call her.

Dear Esmeralda,

I hope this finds you in good health. I am fine.

(That's the way she starts every letter she has ever written in her entire life.)

I keep praying they will find a cure for my dreaded disease before I die of old age. Do you think they will?

Well, I took your advice a while back and died my hair. A older man with a pigtail come in the store the other day and he asked me if that was a wig I was wearing or what. I told him it were not a wig but I did not tell him it was died hair. Do you think I should have told him the whole truth?

About Percy Poteat . . .

(I should've known my mentioning Percy when we talked on the phone would get her ulcers in an uproar.)

I know he teased me a lot but I like to think it was because he liked me. I got a crush on him in eighth grade the year we dropped out of school. He was very smart. He told me he had a photo mind.

As for them jumpers I wore, Mama didn't have no pattern. She made me a white one for Easter and she was hoping it would do for the next Easter. By the next year I had got a little long legged but she said it would do if I didn't bend over. We had dinner on the grounds that Sunday and a Easter egg hunt. I ate standing up and much as I wanted to find the golden egg I excused myself from the hunt.

Is that music director the one they fired from Cold Water Baptist in Springs County? That name Boris Krantz sort of rings a bell with me.

Yours very truly,

Beatrice

I folded the letter and put it in my apron pocket, but the more I thought about it, the more I knew that somehow I had to get Beatrice to wake up and get a life.

As I worked around the house and in the garden that day, possibilities kept running through my mind. Before I sat down, I knew I had better call Beatrice, because once I sit down, it's hard to get up again. I dialed her number, but there was no answer. I figured she wasn't off work yet.

I sat down, and before I knew it, I had fallen asleep. It was eleven o'clock when I came to, too late to call anybody. So I went to bed.

Naturally, a few days went by, and I had not gotten back to Beatrice. At night I would think about calling her, but I would be so tired that I just wasn't up to tackling her main problem, namely Percy Poteat and the dreamworld she was living in. The more I thought about it, the more I convinced myself that writing a letter would be better than talking on the phone. That way I could make sure I was putting it in the best way possible. If I made a mistake, I could change the way I put it. That's not to mention the fact that I would save big bucks by not talking on the phone and also that Beatrice would get a mailbox treat, something besides supermarket coupons to clip.

My tablet was buried under the *Daily Journal,* but I found it and a ballpoint in the drawer.

Dear Beatrice,

I tried to call you but got no answer. The reason I have not wrote is because I have really been hopping here lately. Elijah come and grubbed up the garden. I gave him something extra for Maude and he near 'bout cried. That old man sure loves that old mule and I reckon the mule loves him too.

I had forgot what was in her letter, and since she always asked my advice about things, I dug it out of the basket by my chair. I again was surprised as all get out that she took my advice about her hair.

You must look a lot better with your hair died. Since you had chemo and it come back curly you sure don't need to get another one of them curly perms. I hate them things. As for that man asking you if you wore a wig, no, you don't have to tell him the whole truth. It is nobody's business what you do with your hair.

I sure hope you will let that torch for Percy Poteat flame out. Why, shoot, he never even knew how to say your name. Remember he called you Beetriss. Not Be-AT-trice the way it is spelt.

As for Percy Poteat having a photo mind, he must have run out of film at an early age. Ha! Ha! If you ask me, I think he was light in the upper story. To this day I don't see what you saw in him. Them little round glasses made him look like a owl.

The ballpoint run out of ink, and I had a mischief of a time finding anything to write with. The only thing I could find without getting up was a stub of a pencil in the drawer, so I finished out the letter with that.

Well, Beatrice, the Willing Workers are on the warpath hot and heavy. Boris Krantz has got all the teenagers running after him and Clara says we have got to put the kibosh on that. Mercy me, I say it's better they run after him than some hell-bound rock star. By the way, Clara has already heard about a music director being fired by Cold Water Baptist and you can bet your bottom dollar she's checking to find out if it was Boris they let go. Woe be unto him if it was.

Well, I got to get up from here and do a few things. Let me hear from you.

Your friend,

Esmeralda

I waited to mail the letter until Friday, when I went up to tend to old Mrs. Purdy, because thataway Beatrice would not get it before Monday. If she didn't wait months to answer a letter, she was bad about writing right back. Having shot off my mouth about Percy, I was sure she would answer right away. The more space I could put between mailing that one and getting hers shot right back at me, the better.

3

I guess people think the Willing Workers run the church, and between them and the deacons, in fact, they do. The preacher we've got they take for a wimp. Young and old alike call him Preacher Bob like he has not got a last name nor seminary training to boot. In public I make it my business to call him Reverend Osborne, and in private, Pastor Osborne, and I can tell he appreciates this, though he is not the kind of man to put himself forward. As Splurgeon would say, "He whose worth speaks will not speak his own worth."

The wife he has got was once the saddest looking creature you ever laid eyes on. But she wasn't always like that. When they came to Live Oaks sixteen years ago, she was the prettiest bride ever you saw, and they were both full of pep—full of fun and anxious to do good things here. They worked together like hand in glove. Went knocking on doors and got people in church who had not darkened the doors for years. They really wore themselves out reaching the young people. They'd take them on hikes, hayrides, wiener roasts, summer camps, and such, don't you know. Both of them could sing, but then she quit singing in the choir. I don't know how many young people went off to Bible school because of the Osbornes' work. But a lot of the older people criticized him for spending too much of his time with the young people when there were shut-ins and sick folks he needed to be taking care of.

Back then, Reverend Osborne preached with passion and held street meetings long after that kind of thing was not done anymore. That's when the deacons told him they wanted him to "move along with the times," and little by little, that's what came to pass at Apostolic Bible.

Reverend Osborne didn't cave in, but there were changes in Live Oaks that had a bearing on the way things were going in the church. When the mill closed, people had to move away to find work, so there weren't much point in preaching on the streets if there weren't nobody listening. And as soon as the teenagers needed jobs, they left town, and that was the end of the youth work.

So Pastor Osborne was left having more funerals than weddings, but he didn't leave; he kept right on tending the flock, visiting the sick and holding their hands when they were dying. It wasn't until this new crop of young'uns came along that the deacons decided to hire a music director who could keep the teenyboppers in church.

I watched our preacher through all of this, and to my way of thinking, it seasoned him. People said the light in his study at the church was on late at night. Of course, there was a mean opinion going around that he dreaded going home, but I knew he was in there poring over the Scriptures and books that lined the shelves of that little cubbyhole. It showed in his sermons. We got something to think about or to do every time he spoke, and he never lost sight of Jesus. I believe that's what brought the new high school Spanish teacher to Apostolic. She'd not been born again long, and she drank in that new wine like it was Gatorade. The preacher's critics would've liked to have him lighten up. They would've liked for him to clown around in the pulpit like that preacher at Bethel does, but he didn't. And I, for one, needed that red meat of the Word he gave us.

I have a notion that Pastor Osborne spent a lot of time on his knees. He sure had a lot to pray about, mainly his wife.

Like I said before, Betty Osborne was not the same woman she'd been as a bride. I can't remember exactly how old she was when they came here, but now she was pushing forty, one side or the other, maybe thirty-nine and holding. She bemoaned the fact that they didn't have any children, and like the kudzu vines taking over the abandoned mill, it was eating away at her, just swallowing her whole. The hardest time for her was when her husband dedicated a baby in church. When one of the Neely boys and his wife brought their twins to the front for dedication, Betty burst into tears and ran out of the service.

I couldn't guess whether she had taken them fertilizer treatments or not. She must have, because she had given up on ever having a baby. But I didn't think he had. Why do I say that? Well, there was a young unmarried girl in the next town who got pregnant once, and her family tried to persuade her to give up the baby. Her parents came to the Osbornes and asked them if they would not like to have the child, seeing as how they were good Christians. Then maybe their daughter might come to her senses and be willing to part with her baby when it came. Betty got all excited, but the pastor said they'd have to pray about it. When the family came back again, Reverend Osborne said no, that it would be cruel to take the baby away from its mama if the mama didn't want to let go.

After that, Betty Osborne was not only depressed, she was so mad at him she took her leave and flew off to her mama's and stayed away three weeks.

I'd not say this even to Beatrice, but I figured it was probably his fault they couldn't make babies. That's the kind of thing can make a man lose heart in himself. Make him so sober he don't laugh no more, and although Reverend Osborne would smile, that was about it. Must've been that medicine they advertise on TV for a man's problem didn't work for him, or else he had not tried it. The only doctor we've got here is Dr. Elsie, and it might be because she's a woman that Pastor Osborne goes up to the University Medical Center for his checkups. Dr. Elsie is a good doctor, but she's getting old. When she retires, I doubt we can get another doctor to come here.

Well, now, let me get back to Reverend Osborne (my mind takes a notion now and then to wander all over the place). It's hard to describe the pastor, but I tell you flat out, he is no wimp. Even back when I first knew him, I could tell he was the kind of man who'd make a good father. Kindness is his middle name, and patience is his long suit. Otherwise he would've pulled up stakes long ago and left Apostolic on account of the officers and members he has to deal with here.

The reason I knew he would be a good father was because he had a good father. One time when he was helping me shell pecans, he told me about his daddy—said they were very poor and that his daddy worked two jobs to make a living for his family. But even so, he found the time to be with his boy—played catch with him, took him fishing and such. But mainly it was the things he taught his son. Pastor Osborne said his daddy taught him how to get along with people, how to make his money make do, all kinds of things. Showed him how to always look out for poor people.

When he was telling me about his daddy, I could see in his eyes how much he was wanting a boy of his own. I could understand that, because Bud had always wanted a son. Bud was overseas when our baby was born dead, and when he came back with his mind gone and his body full of shrapnel, there weren't opportunity for us to make another one. Our baby was a boy too. Full term. To this day, I can't think about what a comfort and joy it would be to me if our baby had lived and was now grown to manhood. I just have to put it out of my mind.

I always believed that if Reverend Osborne had a son, he would be a different man. Joy would come back in him. And I tell you, I knew he would grow a boy into a good, solid man like himself.

And since that happened about Betty Osborne running off thataway, the burden for them to have a family never left me. So far nothing had come of all my praying, and it looked like the Lord was going to let her clock run down without giving her any offspring. It sure was hard to understand. Frankly, I didn't.

4

❦

I hate it when people write right back the same day they get my letter. I knew that's what Beatrice would do when she read what I wrote about Percy. It's a wonder she didn't get on the telephone and run up another big bill. Anyway, here's what she wrote:

Dear Esmeralda,

I hope this finds you in good health. I am fine. My feet are killing me. I guess there's no use praying they'll stop hurting. All the praying I have done about a cure for my dreaded disease has not had no answer.

I know you are smarter than me but you don't understand my feelings for Percy. You got to marry your Bud and even though he got wounded and all in the war and wasn't right in his head, at least you got to care for him until he died. But I never got to marry Percy and he's the onliest man I ever wanted to marry. I have heard you say many a time that you married the best and would never look at another man. That's the way I have always felt about Percy.

As for the way he said my name it was his mama's fancy way of talking that had him calling me Beetriss. I kind of liked that. Made me feel like a movie star. It like to have broke my heart when they called Percy into service but the war ended pretty soon after that. Like as not he married some nice girl up north or out west some place.

I have got a framed picture of him and when I got your letter I took it out to look at it. I guess them little round glasses did make him look kinda like a owl. Well, owls are real wise, Esmeralda.

There's a young couple looked at the apartment upstairs. I hope they move in. It will be company for me just hearing them moving about up there.

I'm going on a diet. I have got to trim up that flabby flesh that flaps under my upper arms. It's an easy diet. All I have to do is eat grapefruits and mayo.

I'm praying for the Willing Workers but mostly for Boris Krantz.

Yours very truly,

Beatrice

Well, that letter didn't set right with me. I didn't like her doubting the Lord about a cure for cancer. And I was a little sorry I had made fun of Percy, although for the life of me I couldn't believe she loved him like I'd loved Bud. Percy Poteat couldn't hold a candle to Bud.

The next Friday when I went up to Mrs. Purdy's to clean her house, I saw they were having a yard sale next door, so I took a look. There was a glider for sale, and when the woman came down to my price, I went home. As I had figured, there was enough money in that fruit jar where I keep my savings to pay for it. Every week after I pay tithe and buy groceries, I put what change I've got left in savings. Papa always taught us not to spend all we got but to keep back some. I always made sure I had the price of a bus ticket in case I had to go see about Beatrice. Well, I called Elmer after I got that glider, and he said he'd haul it up to my house as soon as he closed the store.

I still couldn't get Beatrice's letter off my mind. It made me think a lot about Bud and that hateful war that was no war at all, just something the politicians got started and wouldn't stop. I still don't know where Vietnam is, but Bud said it was his duty to go over there and fight the commies. Well, I did a lot of praying with him over there. I thought my faith was strong, but I guess it weren't strong enough. They sent him to one hospital after another until I brought him home. What was left of him was nothing but pain and misery for ten years, eight months.

If Elijah had not helped me, I couldn't have took care of Bud. Elijah would come over here and bathe him, help me get him in the car, do whatever I needed him to do. When Bud would get crazy and start hollering and tearing up the house, the only person could calm him down was Elijah. Many a night I'd call Elmer, and he'd go get Elijah and bring him up here. I'd get out of the room and leave it to him. By the time Elijah would get Bud quieted down, it would be daylight. I'd peek in the room and see the two of them in that old rocker, Elijah humming and holding Bud in his arms like a baby, rocking him back and forth.

I never could think about that without filling up, so I pulled myself together and thought about Beatrice.

It took a few days before I got a handle on Beatrice. I knew I'd hurt her feelings about Percy, but mercy me, I was the only person in the whole wide world who had a chance of easing her out of that fantasy. On the other hand, I figured maybe a dream was better than nothing at all.

The next time I was in the hardware store, I asked Elmer about Percy, and I got news that I knew might break Beatrice's heart. I wasn't sure if I should or could tell her.

As for a cure for cancer, I needed to say something to buck up her faith. But in my heart I felt like a hypocrite. Nothing any preacher, even Reverend Osborne, had ever said helped me understand for sure why my prayers for Bud weren't answered. When he went overseas, I asked the Lord a million times to keep him safe, and when he came home without his mind and his body shot through with shrapnel, I asked the Lord to heal him, even though I didn't have much faith he would. And he didn't.

Now here I was, getting ready to tell Beatrice God would send a cure for America's Most Wanted killer, even though that killer still escapes the minds of the best brains in the country.

Well, needless to say, I didn't feel ready to tackle all this, but I finally picked up the phone.

It rang three times before Beatrice answered. She sounded down.

"What's the matter?" I asked.

"My tongue is turning black. It scares the daylights outta me."

"Well, I should think it would!"

"I'm scairt to death. Do you think my dreaded disease is coming back on me?"

"No, I do not," I said, although I was not so sure. That killer can show up anywhere. "Your tongue is turning black because you've been on that fool diet. You deserve to be sick unto death! You of all people do not need to be on a diet. You don't hardly cast a shadder as it is. Leave off the grapefruits and mayo and eat nothing but fresh vegetables, cornbread, and buttermilk until you get straightened out."

"Are you sure that's what it is?"

"As sure as rain," I lied. Well, maybe it wasn't a lie; it hadn't rained in a month of Sundays.

"Beatrice," I said, "I don't want to run up a big bill here, so let me say what I have to say real quick and get off the line. Don't you dare give up praying for that cure."

(Anybody use the word *cancer* with Beatrice, she would panic and get historical.)

"It's a big thing you're asking for and it takes a whole lot of trust. And a lot of patience, I might add. In his own time and in his own way, the Lord will give a cure if it's his will. As Splurgeon says, 'He pleases God best who trusts him most.'"

"I know you're right, Esmeralda, but it's so hard to wait. You don't hear people praying much these days, do you?"

"No, you don't," I said as I was trying to straighten out the twisted phone cord. "Remember when the Willing Workers were gung ho about writing letters to the president to get him to put prayer back in the schools? My question was then and it is now: When are they going to put prayer back in the church? You remember how Wednesday nights used to be at Apostolic—young and old alike flocking to prayer meeting. There was such good singing and testimonies and prayer requests. Remember how John Williams always took up more time than all the rest of us put together testifying and wanting us to pray for all the souls he was trying to win?"

"I remember. Before he'd get started, Pastor McBrayer would always tell him to make it short."

"Little good it did, but I tell you, we all loved to hear John Williams pray! We'd all get down on our knees, remember? First one, then another would pray, but sometimes John would pray twice. Nowadays nobody gets down on their knees. Wonder how they'll do on that day when every knee shall bow and every tongue confess? Ha! Ha!"

"Don't the Catholics and Episcopalians kneel?"

"Well, you got me there." I got the cord untangled, but it didn't stay that way long. "Now, Beatrice, you know I have got to cut this short, but do you remember that little motto tacked up on the wall: MUCH PRAYER, MUCH POWER; LITTLE PRAYER, LITTLE POWER; NO PRAYER, NO POWER? Well, it has come to that. No prayer to speak of and no power, just Wednesday night suppers and activities."

"It's a sin and a shame, ain't it?"

"Yes, it is, but we mustn't give up. Oh, by the way, I got most of the garden planted, and to tell the truth, at day's end all I want to do is sit on the porch and rest. I used my savings to buy me a nice glider at a yard sale, and Elmer brought it up to the house. He didn't want to take pay, so I told him to go down in the basement and take whatever jars of the canned stuff he wanted. I got jars dating back three or four years. He was tickled to death."

Throughout this conversation, I was debating back and forth whether or not to tell Beatrice what I had learned about Percy. Finally I figured I had put it off as long as I could. It wouldn't be right not to tell her, but breaking the news wouldn't be easy. I hoped the Lord would help me say it.

I tried to sound sympathetic. "Beatrice, your letter made me think about you and Percy. I guess I didn't really know how you felt about him." I paused, wondering if I should apologize in case I had hurt her feelings. I didn't know what to do, seeing as I was about to drop a bombshell on her and all. So I just took a deep breath and dived in. "Beatrice," I said, "I hope you won't mind that I took it upon myself to find out what's happened to Percy . . ."

I figured the poor girl might just climb through the telephone when she heard that! I continued all in a rush. "Elmer said he heard Percy first married a Veetnamese and after that a Yankee and after that another woman."

I thought I heard her suck in her breath. But I didn't hear nothing else. She was so quiet, I went on talking about other things for a while so as not to leave her so upset.

"Now that the weather's nice, the homeless are camping in the grove again. Of course, most of them have got homes, they just don't want to live by the rules in that home. Well, I'll tell you, I think they hide out in the grove because they're afraid they might see a sign that says 'Now Hiring.' Boris takes food down there every Saturday morning—whatever's left over from the men's fellowship breakfast at church."

When I paused, I thought I heard her murmur, "That's nice," probably hoping I wouldn't detect she was crying.

I kept on talking. "By the way, Boris has won over Clara. He asked her granddaughter to play the violin in morning service, and that was all it took. Clara has dropped her Cold Water Baptist investigation. . . . Did I tell you Boris started a bell choir? Them bells play the mischief with hearing aids."

Well, finally, I just had to hang up. "I got to go, Beatrice. Let me know if your tongue don't get better."

I sat in my chair a long time, wondering if I had done the right thing. I hated hurting her, but if the hurt would put an end to her pining over Percy, then maybe she could get on with her life. That poor girl never had much love of any kind. Her daddy run off when she was a baby, and her mama died young. As a child she never even had a pet dog or cat. That's probably why she loved that old tomcat the way she did. That was the most spoiled animal in the U.S. of A.

As I sat there thinking about Beatrice, a lump got stuck in my throat. I had to fight back the tears. "Lord," I said, "can't you bring somebody into Beatrice's life besides me who will love her?"

I knew that was a big order and not likely to happen, but it seemed like the only decent thing I could do, now that I had done in Percy.

5

I didn't hear from Beatrice for a long time. Several times I thought about calling her. I had a good excuse— I could just say I was calling to see if her tongue was still black. Of course, I knew she was well or I would've heard different.

So I went about my business, even though I still worried about her. I did kind of get her off my mind when I went to church one Wednesday night, because the trouble with that music man made me put Beatrice on the back burner.

The latest with Boris Krantz was that he weren't satisfied with the piano and organ we worked so hard to pay for. He had to have that backup music on tape. We would sit there on pins and needles while he fiddled with the machine, and the youth choir would stand waiting for him to get the tape started at the right place. It would get going, and they would start singing all this music that comes straight out of Nashville. And if that weren't bad enough, one Sunday he had a young boy, who was not a member of our church, play the guitar. Only he couldn't half play.

As I saw it, the Willing Workers wouldn't stand for much of that nonsense once they caught on to what Boris was up to. Little by little, he was sneaking in a full-fledged band like they got down at Bethel Church. First a guitar, next thing there'd be a drummer banging away and all kinds of brass horns blasting eardrums and personally driving me up the wall.

I tell you, it seemed to me the world was coming into the church, and it was coming in fast! I was sure it was all this good economy we were having. Hard times is better for keeping folks close to the Lord. Like Splurgeon says, "If we have nothing but prosperity, we will be burned up with worldliness." I tell you, Apostolic Bible Church was beginning to smell of the smoke of worldliness!

Enough of that. Much to my relief, I finally did get a three-page letter from Beatrice, but there was not a word in it about Percy. I was shocked. What did that mean? Was she mad at me? Was she over him? Had she cooked up some other crazy explanation, like the reason he had got married three times was because he really loved her and didn't know it? I tell you, Beatrice did not live in the real world!

Well, what she did write was that her tongue was better and she was sticking to fresh vegetables and buttermilk. "To tell the truth," she wrote, "I was getting sick of that mayo."

Well, who wouldn't!

"I am not sleeping good at all," she continued.

The couple that moved in upstairs come home from their honeymoon fighting and they've been fighting like cats and dogs ever since. All that yelling and slamming doors is like to drive me crazy.

That's the way it always was with Beatrice; if it wasn't one thing, it was another.

As if all that fighting was not enough, my feet are killing me. A rich lady come in the store yesterday and she saw me rubbing my one foot. She told me my feet hurt from standing on that concrete floor and she gave me the card of somebody she said I should go see. He has a foreign name and he is a p-o-d-i-a-t-r-i-s-t. I don't know what that is. Like as not he is one of them gurus or sighkicks. I am not about to go to one of them.

Esmeralda, when I think of Christians like Mr. Splurgeon, I feel so useless. He never went to Apostolic Bible, did he? I could never do all he did, but I wish there was something I could do for the Lord.

Yours very truly,

Beatrice

I was busy as all get out, but seeing as how she was overrun with stuff she couldn't handle, I took the time to write right back to her.

Dear Beatrice,

As for your feet you have probably got bunions right and left. Every night soak your feet in warm Epsom salts. The onliest doctor you need is Dr. Scholl. You will find his stuff in any decent drugstore and he don't send bills. Ha! Ha! Get yourself some of them footpads that will hold up your archers and leave them bunions room to breathe. You better hurry. Like as not any day now them HMOs who want a monopoly on health care will find a way to outlaw Dr. Scholl!

As for finding something to do for the Lord, Beatrice, I say we do everything for the Lord.

You asked me about Mr. Splurgeon. No, he don't go to Apostolic Bible. He had a tabernacle up in Baltimore or some place away from here. I think he's dead now. The picture in the book shows he was too fat and he smoked, so most likely he is pushing up daisies. Bud's mama gave him this Splurgeon book and I have near about memorized it. Bud loved that book. Even after he came home from the war and his brain had left him, whenever he had to go to the veterans hospital I would take his Bible and the Splurgeon book with us. I have put it in my will that when I die Splurgeon's book will go to Reverend Osborne.

I'd write more but I've got to get up to Mrs. Purdy's. You remember old Mrs. Purdy lives up on the hill. Lost her eyesight a few years back. Her cat got gone and Elmer said he had sent his part-time help up there to look all over the neighborhood for it. It's been gone five days, he said. Well, it don't look like Flossie Ann is coming back and if she don't that'll be the death of Mrs. Purdy. I'm going up there to see what I can do. I read my Bible this morning and prayed I'd find that cat but it is not likely. Splurgeon says, "Hear God and He will hear you," so I'm just counting on that. I got to go now.

Esmeralda

When I got up the hill, I found poor old Mrs. Purdy just sitting in her chair, grieving her heart out. As I went about washing her dishes and cleaning up the kitchen, she kept calling me.

"Esmeralda, never mind the housework, just find my precious Flossie Ann."

"I'm looking," I'd say, and I was. But I had serious doubts that I'd ever find her, especially alive. As I scrubbed the floors, vacuumed, and dusted—all the while I was doing them things—I was looking in cabinets and closets and so forth, hoping I wouldn't find a stiff corpse but that Flossie Ann would pop out at me, alive and well. I went down in the basement, then up in the attic, but there was no sign of that cat.

I was about to give up, thinking my worst fears had come true—that Flossie Ann was pasted on the road someplace. I started asking the Lord that since it was not his will to let me find her, would he please give me the words to ease Mrs. Purdy's broke heart.

But then I went back in the spare bedroom to straighten out the dresser drawers and pulled out the bottom one. Lo and behold, there was Flossie Ann! She looked up at me, her eyes pitiful enough to make a grown man cry.

"I found her!" I hollered, and as I gently gathered her up in my arms, I could hear Mrs. Purdy shouting, "Thank you, Jesus! Thank you, Jesus!"

That cat was so bony that I wrapped a towel around her so as not to hurt her. Then I carried the little thing to the living room, where Mrs. Purdy was reaching out with both arms. The minute she touched Flossie Ann, she grabbed her out of my hands and hugged her so close I was afraid she'd kill the poor creature.

I wish you could have seen them two—Mrs. Purdy just a-bawling and a-laughing at the same time, and Flossie Ann looking up at her kind of cross-eyed, too weak to meow.

"Where'd you find her?" Mrs. Purdy asked. I told her I'd found Flossie Ann in a drawer. She commenced to feeling the cat all over. "She's too warm. How does she look?"

"A mite skinny," I told her, "but she'll not die. You better let me have her, Mrs. Purdy. She needs taking care of."

"That's right. Here, you take her." And she lifted Flossie Ann ever so gently. "See that she gets plenty of water. Where's my cane? . . . Thank you kindly. You go along, I'll get there in a minute or two."

I took Flossie Ann to the kitchen to feed her. She was too weak to drink by herself, so I got the meat-basting thing, filled it with water, and put it to her mouth.

Mrs. Purdy tapped her way into the kitchen. "Esmeralda, what do you think?"

"She's wobbly, Mrs. Purdy, but I'll see to it she gets over this."

It took a while, but as soon as Flossie Ann had all the water she wanted, I eased her down on the floor. "Now, Mrs. Purdy, can't I fix you some oatmeal or something?"

"Well, now, I reckon you can. Guess I ain't et much in I don't know how long."

That was no surprise to me. "I'd say it's near about as many days as Flossie Ann's been missing."

"You're probably right." She felt for the chair and sat down at the table. "Seems like I should've heard her calling me in that drawer."

"Oh, now, Mrs. Purdy, you and me both have got hearing loss."

Oatmeal cooks fast, and after I'd served Mrs. Purdy a bowl of it, I put the brown sugar and milk where she could reach it. Then I went back to the bedroom to make sure there was no mess in that drawer. It wasn't too bad, so I cleaned it up and was about to come out the door when I spotted a 1958 calendar on the wall. There was a picture of the Grand Canyon on it that was still in good condition, so I asked Mrs. Purdy if I could have it. Of course, she said I could.

Beatrice had always talked about going to the Grand Canyon, and I knew she'd just love the picture. Which, I figured, was about as close as she'd ever get to the real thing.

I was tired when I got home that day. I flopped in my chair and thought, *Oh me of little faith,* because for once I could see the Lord had really answered my prayer about finding that cat. But what bothered me was that he didn't seem to answer the big things in life. Having prayed my heart out for Bud to come back from the war safe and sound and him winding up like he did was something I would never understand. And the thing about the preacher and his wife not having a baby when all over the country women were doing away with babies before they were born, I would never understand.

I knew all the things people said about unanswered prayer, like "You have not got enough faith." Well, my faith might've been the size of a grain of mustard seed (I knew I had got that much, maybe more), but Jesus said this much planted in God was enough. People would argue that if your prayer be not answered, there was something wrong in your life. But not a day went by that I didn't ask the Lord to forgive me for any sin I'd committed, and I knew he wiped the slate clean. "The Lord is testing you," people would say, but my Bible told me God don't tempt nobody. Or people would say, "Just wait." Well, I waited till the day Bud died for the Lord to do something for him, and all I got was a flat-out no!

As soon as I let that thought slip out, I was sorry. Of course, the Lord knew I was mad about it. He knew my heart. He still does, and when I flare up like that, I'm always sorry.

It's just that sometimes I can't leave it be, Lord.

I sighed, weary with thinking about it.

6

I love my Sundays! I start getting ready on Saturday night—lay out the clothes I'm going to wear, see that they are pressed, wash and roll up my hair. While it dries, I read my Sunday school lesson.

Since it was not raining the Sunday after I found Flossie Ann, I walked to church. In class, Clara didn't take up all the time telling us who was sick and all, so we had a pretty decent lesson.

I tell you, Pastor Osborne's morning prayer always takes me right up to heaven, and that morning was no exception. His morning prayer isn't one of them that gives the Lord a shopping list of who's sick or in the hospital. He starts off with worshiping the Lord, then moves on to blessing the congregation from the little children right on up to the elders and deacons. He always prays for those in authority over us, the president right on down to the mayor. You would think he has the newspaper open before him, the way he prays for crimes to be solved, for missing children, for prisoners on death row, for victims of storms and accidents. Missionaries get prayed for by name, and their needs get mentioned. Then on different Sundays he takes turns praying for teachers, policemen, doctors, and nurses—all the like of that. That morning he prayed for two Hollywood celebrities who were in trouble.

After a prayer like that, my heart was ready to hear the message, and what a message it was! He spoke on tears and sighs. I wondered what he would get out of that until he explained that tears and sighs are sometimes our best prayers. His text came from Exodus, the part when the children of Israel were in bondage and suffering so bad, and the Lord told them, "I have heard thy prayer, I have seen thy tears." Oh, it was wonderful! After all, hasn't every one of us been at that place where we hardly know how to pray anymore and we just flood our pillows with tears?

Pastor Osborne said David once prayed that the Lord would put his tears in a bottle. To me that meant that David didn't want the Lord to forget whatever it was he wept over. I didn't know where David got the idea of the bottle, but Pastor Osborne explained that women collected their tears in a container of some kind and maybe those were the tears Mary used to wash Jesus' feet.

I just marveled at that man. You never got one of them quickie sermons off the top of his head like some preachers would give you.

People in my church are quick to clap at any little thing like they were watching TV or some entertainment, but that morning the Spirit was moving, and you could hear a pin drop.

While he was talking, I found myself wishing he had used that verse, "They that sow in tears shall reap in joy." Pastor Osborne never fails to sow the good seed of the Word of God at Apostolic, but with hard hearts and minds made up, it hasn't always been easy. But he was and still is a real soul-winner who goes after the drunks and wife-beaters as well as the top dogs in town. I bet he's watered that seed real good with his tears. I hope I live long enough for that morning when he reaps with joy.

I think he got his verses on sighing from the Book of Lamentations, which is full of doom and gloom. When you can't pray and you sigh a lot, Reverend Osborne said Jesus is listening and hears them sighs as if they were words. I remember reading in one of the Gospels that Jesus sighed himself, so I guess he knows good and well what a sigh means.

I needed to go to the bathroom, but I tell you, I did not want that sermon to end. As far as I was concerned, he could've gone on all day. But he wound it up in the sweetest kind of way. He quoted a verse from Revelation, telling us our prayers go up before the throne of the Lord as incense, a sweet-smelling fragrance that fills heaven.

Can you beat that? Made me want to come right home and get on my knees. As we filed out of church, I shook Reverend Osborne's hand, but I could hardly speak I was so full. He took me aside and leaned down close to my ear to speak privately. "You know, Esmeralda, when I was a young man entering the ministry, my pastor told me, 'Robert, always speak to the broken hearts. There's one in every pew.' When I started out preaching, I didn't pay much attention to that. I guess a man has to have a broken heart himself before he can . . ." His voice cracked, and he let go my hand.

Now I know people might say a man of the cloth ought to be able to live above his disappointments and so forth. Maybe he should, but he's human too, the same as me. One thing is sure: Pastor Osborne didn't put on a happy face and pretend he had not got a care in the world, like the hypocrites do.

I had invited Boris to come for Sunday dinner so I could talk to him about that Nashville music, but after hearing Pastor Osborne's sermon, I was glad he didn't come. I wanted to be by myself.

Well, somebody had invited Boris to be their guest at the restaurant. After morning service, the church crowd always goes to the all-you-can-eat restaurant here in town. Once, one of the waitresses told me she hates to see them come in.

"They forget their manners, if they have any," she said. "It's 'Miss' this and 'Miss' that. You can't fill up their tea glasses fast enough. And there's one lady always says she ordered something else, not what I brought her. And there are others who'll say the food is cold or too salty. There's one man always asks if the mashed potatoes are made with instant potatoes, when he ought to know by now that's the only kind we serve. You would think after what they put me through, they would all leave a big tip. I do well to get fifty cents from some of them, but I get tracts every Sunday. I tell you, Esmeralda, if that crowd would eat at home on Sundays, maybe I could get off now and then to go to church myself."

I'm glad I don't go out to eat with that crowd; they would embarrass me to death. Papa brought us up to remember the Sabbath day and to keep it holy. I don't condemn anybody for eating out and shopping on Sunday, mind you, but I can't do it. For me, it's a sin. Besides, like I say, I love my Sundays.

For dinner I had a pot roast with onions and gravy, real mashed potatoes, slaw, and green beans cooked the way Mama always cooked them, with seasoning. And I made good biscuits and ice tea that has got the flavor it is meant to have.

After I ate and cleaned up the kitchen, I flopped in my recliner. Started to read my Bible but couldn't keep my eyes open. So I took a little nap. That refreshed me, and when I woke up, I felt like singing.

Over a lifetime I have sung the same hymns so many times I can sing all the verses without looking at the book. Right now, if I was to call up Beatrice and ask her what hymn is on page fifty, without looking, she could tell me "Great Is Thy Faithfulness." Or if I asked, "Page ninety-four?" she could tell me in a skinny minute it is "At Calvary." In fact, we sung them two so much the pages have fell out the book.

I can't always sing around the house when I'm working, but sometimes I do. If anybody was to hear me, they'd probably think I was hog calling. But on Sunday

I rear back in this chair and sing to my heart's content. I never get tired of singing, but my main business on Sunday afternoon is to get in a lot more praying than I get done weekdays. True, sometimes my mind wanders and I start thinking about other things. I hate that.

If I was talking to somebody visiting me, I sure wouldn't be looking out the window or over their shoulder at somebody or something else. That would be impolite. But with the Lord, well, if you've ever done much praying, you've had the same experience, I'm sure. I'll tell you one way that helps ease my conscience. I tell myself that whatever my mind wanders off to, that's something I ought to be praying about. And I sometimes pray out loud. That's beginning to come natural with me, because to tell the truth, I feel like the Lord is right here with me some Sunday afternoons. Even when I don't feel it, I believe he's here.

By the time I finished my Bible reading, I didn't have time to read Splurgeon. I had to get up and get ready for evening service.

By the middle of the week, I had a letter from Beatrice, and wouldn't you know it, she mentioned about how her mind wanders when she's praying.

In the letter, she didn't mention her foot problem, so she must've gotten over that.

Dear Esmeralda,

I hope this finds you in good health. I am fine. I am not sleeping much before one or two o'clock in the morning because of them two upstairs. That gives me a lot of time to think. I pray for them but my mind wanders. There's just so long you can pray for somebody.

I went to preaching this morning and there were some young people playing musical instruments and singing songs they must of made up. They would sing a line or two and then repeat it over and over again. They sang good and they looked so clean and happy. I guess their music is like what they listen to on the radio and that's all they know. For me I wish they sang "In the Garden." Mama used to sing that even when she was so sick she couldn't get up anymore.

A lot of people object to all of this new music. They say it's too much like rock and roll. It's like when we were young and sang some jazzy choruses the old people didn't like.

I don't know if I am right about this or not but I got to thinking that music is like a language. Everybody don't speak the same language. If a missionary was to go to China he couldn't just speak English, he'd have to learn to speak Chinese, wouldn't he? If somebody is trying to reach young people today, wouldn't he have to use their kind of music?

Well, I don't know how to explain it good, but do you understand what I'm trying to say? I know you are smarter than me, but this just come to me sitting there in church thinking about *Mama* singing *"In the Garden."*

Yours very truly,

Beatrice

P.S. I'm glad Boris Krantz won over Clara. Maybe the W. W.s won't run him off after all.

Well, I never thought I'd live to see the day when Beatrice Thompson would set me back on my heels like she did with that letter. I was so glad Boris did not come for Sunday dinner, because I would've shot off my mouth about the new music. I saw then that I would've been dead wrong. What Beatrice said about music made good sense, and good sense is not something comes natural with her.

All day long, I turned it over and over in my mind, arguing this way and that, but every argument I had was trumped by what she wrote. Seeing I couldn't win, I guessed that the Lord was in this thing. That letter coming in the nick of time to keep me from making a fool of myself was nothing less than God's providence, and I knew I better not be stubborn about giving in.

I have to laugh now when I think about it. Imagine Beatrice Thompson setting me straight!

I still don't like that kind of music, but I keep my mouth shut about it. Pastor Osborne does see to it that we sing hymns. His favorite is "A Mighty Fortress Is Our

God." I like that one, but my favorite is "How Firm a Foundation."

Well, I got to go hoe the garden. Like every summer, it seems, it's been so dry even the weeds have not got the heart to grow. The best they can do is wiggle out the ground, then keel over. Ha! Ha!

7

The fat was in the fire! Elijah's mule fell sick, and he come to Reverend Osborne to ask him to pray for Maude. Well, Reverend Osborne did, and when the W.W.s heard tell of it, they went ballistic! They said they never heard of nobody praying for a mule.

Well, I stood up for Pastor Osborne and Elijah and especially Maude. I opened up telling how I prayed for Flossie Ann and how I found her in the dresser drawer. I told them I for one knew it was A-OK to pray for any mule, cow, hog, dog—any of God's creatures.

Seeing I was winning, I let them in on the fact that Splurgeon thought animals went to heaven, not because they were saved but because they were God's creations and they belonged to him. Boy, did that raise a hullabaloo!

They said flat out they didn't believe me, and I told them they were in no position to argue with Mr. Spurgeon, who was a great man of God.

Clara got so loud, you could hear her in the next county. "You mean to tell me you think there's dogs and cats running around in heaven?"

And prissy Mabel Elmwood piped up, "If there's a dog in heaven, I'm not going up there. I'm scared to death of dogs."

There was no use arguing with them. That Yankee, Thelma, grinning like a Cheshire cat, asked, "Do all animals go to heaven, or do some of them go to hell?"

Well, I told her I did not know, because I'd never been there. I felt like saying, "Maybe you can check that out when you go." But I didn't. Instead, I picked up my pocketbook, Bible, and quarterly and left before the bell rang.

I knew those women would spend the rest of the class period talking about it not being right to pray for animals. I tell you, I wanted no part of it. I knew where I stood. I also knew that as soon as the W.W.s got home, my phone would ring off the hook.

Sure enough, as soon as they all got home from the restaurant, they started calling. Every one of them started out mealymouthed, saying they were sorry if they had hurt my feelings. But I knew them women. I knew that was not the reason they were calling me. Because they were all agreed I was wrong and they were right; they were feeling their oats and wanted to keep on enjoying their win.

I could tell they had all got in on it together, because they repeated their comments in the same words. They said the preacher had not only prayed for Maude, he had called the vet and paid out of his own pocket to have the vet take a look at her. That, they said, was putting feet to his prayer, which was not faith at all. Besides, where'd he get money to spend like that?

Those women made me tired. They wouldn't go to the preacher and have anything out with him. They were afraid they might learn something, I guess. If truth be known, they stood in awe of him. They knew what Reverend Osborne was, and down in their hearts, they must've known what they were. They had all got tongues that flapped at both ends and talked behind his back, stirring up trouble.

Well, I would have no part of it, and I told them I was praying for Maude too, and what did they think of that?

Thelma, for one, hung up on me.

Before I could get down to Elijah's and see about Maude, she died. I decided not to put Elijah on the prayer chain, but somebody did, and they all came to me, asking what the W.W.s should do. I told them I was making some stew beef and rice and that they were welcome to come along with me to take it to poor Elijah.

Oh, but I knew what they were thinking. I knew good and well what they were thinking—that Maude dying proved it was wrong to pray for animals. That would come out sooner or later; when it did, I'd be ready for them.

Clara insisted on driving, and we all piled in her car with my stew beef and biscuits and cobbler somebody else had made. Elijah lives down on the branch that runs under the old Southern tracks. Clara took a wrong turn on a dirt road, and we wound up above his place alongside the tracks. An old yeller boxcar was on a siding, and there was three little children sitting on a pile of railroad ties. We told them to go on home, but they just looked at us like they weren't going anyplace. Thelma said they didn't speak English. Well, I couldn't agree. Since they spoke not a word, how did she know? But what I did know was that they were too little to be by themselves. Some grown-up was nearby, probably relieving themself, I said.

We had a mischief of a time scrambling down the embankment to get to Elijah's place. We dared not hold on to each other for fear we'd all wind up in a heap at the bottom. Elijah was sitting under the chinaberry tree with his head in his hands. We took the food inside, and when I came out to see about him, he looked up. He was so pitiful, crying just the way he did when Bud died. When I saw them trails of tears on his old dusky cheeks, I put my arms around him and hugged him good. Then I asked him to come inside, since the ladies wanted to visit with him.

As you might suspect, when I was warming up the stew beef and rice, Clara sided up to me and took me to task about how it was not proper for a white woman to hug a colored man. I apologized and said sweetly that I never noticed he was colored. That jerked a knot in her! Someday I'm going to tell her how many a time Elijah has sat at my dinner table. That will give her a dying duck fit.

Yes, Elijah has sat at my table, and I would not have it any other way. After the way he looked after Bud, what kind of a Christian would I be if I did not count him as a family friend? Why, he never left the room before he got down on his knees and prayed for Bud and me. And since Bud died, Elijah has helped me all he can. He taught me how to plant by the signs and how to tell the weather, all of which my own dear papa never took the time to teach me.

Well, Elijah was so tore up and shaking so bad, I knew there was more than Maude's dying troubling him. I had to do something, so I asked him why he was shaking. He said the city was coming to take Maude and that he was afraid they would sell her to the meat-packing plant to cut her up in little pieces for dog food. I told him not to worry, that I would take care of everything.

And I did.

I passed the word to all the W.W.s that we were to stay put until that truck came. We were all standing outside Elijah's place when the truck rolled up with a white driver and four black men workers with shovels. I marched right up to the cab of that truck and introduced myself and the W.W.s He said he was Horace. Well, I didn't need no introduction. I knew who he was; he was the sheriff's son.

I began my speech by telling him I was a personal friend of the city manager, Roger Elmwood, who also was an elder in our church. "Furthermore," I said, "his wife would be standing here with us, but she declined our invitation due to health reasons. These W.W. ladies and me are here to see to it that Maude—she's the mule—is not sold to the dog-food plant."

He grinned. "Well, ma'am, I'll have to see about that." He rolled up the window and got on the radio to call headquarters. All the time he was on the radio, he was laughing like this was some big joke. He stayed on the line for more time than I liked. When he finally hung up, he grinned and said, "Don't worry about it, ma'am. We'll see this mule gets a decent burial."

Well, I was not fool enough to take him at his word. I told him that me and the W.W.s were going to follow his truck and see to it he done what he said.

I could see he didn't like that one bit. Too bad for him.

It was Clara's car, so I couldn't take Elijah along. But that was just as well, I guess. Horace drove that truck through town like a house afire, no doubt thinking he could shake us. But Clara had put Thelma behind the wheel, and Thelma stayed right on his bumper every turn he made. After swinging back and forth all over town, we finally wound up at the garbage dump.

We piled out, the city workers piled out, and then we just stood there like it was a face-off at a basketball game, them leaning on their shovels and us all in a row.

Horace jumped down from the cab, red in the face. "This is no place for you ladies! You are every one trespassing on city property! Whyn't you all go on home before you get arrested?"

Well, it dawned on me then that not only was Horace the sheriff's son, but in addition to driving the city truck, he was made the deputy by his daddy, which meant he took two bites out of our tax money. I realized this man could make trouble for us, but I didn't share this with the other ladies. We had no choice but to stick by our guns, even if he radioed for help and dragged us off to the city jail. As for Roger Elmwood backing us up, we couldn't count on that unless it was good for him politically.

As Horace fumed, the laborers turned their faces away, thoroughly enjoying the standoff. Finally, Horace said, "Get going with those shovels, men."

After they had dug a hole about three feet deep, he said they could stop.

"Oh, no," Thelma said. "That won't do. Dogs will dig poor Maude up. You've got to dig down—how far, Esmeralda?"

"Ten feet or more."

The workmen looked at Horace, hoping he'd say no. I tell you, he looked like he might. But he just started cursing, calling us names and kicking at the dirt.

I wanted to give him a piece of my mind, but I bit my tongue. Finally, he swore again, looked disgusted, and climbed back in the cab.

That just goes to show you that what Splurgeon said is true: "If a donkey brays at you, you don't have to bray back."

The men would dig a little, then stop to wipe sweat. From time to time, they all slacked up, resting on their shovels. But we didn't say anything, and seeing as Horace was not getting out of the cab, they'd go back to digging.

The sun was getting low by the time it looked like they had dug deep enough. All of us women peered over the hole, and when each one had nodded their approval, Clara told the workers they could stop digging and go get Maude.

By the time they unloaded Maude and dumped her in the hole, it was getting late, but we dared not leave. We waited until every spade of dirt had filled up the grave. Then I went to the cab and told Horace we would be back every day to make sure Maude was not dug up again. He spit out the window, revved up the motor, and after the workers had climbed aboard, he roared back to town.

Late as it was, we all trooped back to Elijah's to tell him he could rest easy. He kept thanking us over and over again.

On the way back to town, we were feeling so good we stopped at the Dairy Queen for a dip. As we sat around talking and laughing, we felt proud. We women get a kick out of bossing men around.

8

We had high winds the Monday after we buried Maude but no rain, and the phone went out. Beatrice tried to call me and panicked even more when she couldn't get through. She scribbled me a note, stuffed a clipping from the newspaper in the envelope, and mailed it overnight express! In the note she said she was shaking all over, which, with all her fears, was nothing new.

It don't look like I will live long enough for my dreaded disease to come back on me. Yesterday up in Springs County two masked men come in a gas station and killed the old man who was running it. They got clean away and chances are they are headed this way. I have no doubt in the world but what I am next on their hit list. Every car rolls up I duck down behind the cig counter and peep out to see if they are wearing masks.

Esmeralda, if you should read in the paper that I been shot, remember you promised to look after my estate. You will find my will right between the mattress and the box springs.

A pickup has just drove up.

This is wrote later. It was the pigtail man who comes in to buy coffee. Drives that truck with a sign on it, Insect Killer Company. Most likely insects is not what he has on his mind. For all I know he is a cereal killer.

Yours very truly,

Beatrice

P.S. I will see you in heaven if I can find you.

I read the details in the newspaper story and found out that man who got killed was not old, he was just my age. I was sorry he got gunned down, but, of course, my main worry was Beatrice. She was in that store alone most of the time, and it was that kind of store gets robbed time and time again.

The phone got fixed that very day, so I called her up. When she used to get herself in a panic, first thing I would do was joke around, hoping that would help her get a grip. "Beatrice, if fears were dollar bills, you would be right up there with them lottery winners," I said. "You don't need to worry about getting killed by a bullet. A masked man come in your station, I guarantee you will drop dead before he can fire off a shot. Ha! Ha! Besides, that holdup happened a couple or three days ago, and Springs County is just across the river. If they were on their way to rob you, they must've got lost or run in the river. Mr. Splurgeon says, 'Fear God and you got nothing else to fear.' Now get over it, honey!"

"That's easy for you to say, Esmeralda," Beatrice said with a big sigh, "but if you were in this store all day by yourself, facing such danger as this, you would not be laughing. I just shake all over."

"I would not be shaking all over. I would be trusting the Lord and taking no chances. Tell you what, when you get off the phone, draw yourself a full tub of warm water and take a long bath. Then drink some warm milk and go to bed."

"I'm out of milk."

I ignored her and went on to the next thing I always would do to calm her down. I changed the subject like I wasn't concerned about the danger she was in. I told her about Maude dying, but I didn't give her all the details. To tell the truth, I was too nervous to go into all of that.

So I said, "Beatrice, quit worrying about that termite man. He's just loafing to pass the time."

I was running out of things to say, but I had to keep her on the line until she felt better.

I began again and tried to sound lighthearted. "Let me tell you about Clara," I said. "Clara is deaf as a post but won't think about getting a hearing aid. I don't understand people who are too vain to wear hearing aids. They don't know what they're missing. A hearing aid will give you the edge, I tell you. Mine picks up sounds I have not heard in years. I can hear every stomach that growls, and when Boris lets go with that Nashville sound, I can tune out. On my pew, all the heads are gray and all them hearing aids whistle, sometimes together, sometimes not. Either way, we're a lot better sounding than them bell ringers. Ha! Ha!"

Beatrice was not laughing.

I remembered the couple upstairs. "You say that young couple fights all the time? Well, you can do something about that. Either you can ask the landlord to evict them or you can ask Jesus to show you how to help them. Maybe that's the very reason the Lord put them upstairs there, so you could help them."

Beatrice wasn't listening. "If I should get shot," she said, "you will take care of my estate, won't you, Esmeralda?"

"Of course, I will, Beatrice, but you are not going to get shot. Tell the Lord how scared you are, and he'll send a flock of angels to camp all around you."

"Do you really think he will?"

"I know he will."

When I hung up, I thought I'd better put Beatrice on the prayer chain. All I had to do was call Thelma, tell her, and she would pass the request on until all the W.W.s got the word. I admit, I was worried about Beatrice. Christians get shot, the same as others. Look at what happened to Bud. Look at what's happening to Christians all over the world being tortured and killed for Jesus.

That whole day, I couldn't get Beatrice off my mind for one minute. I wondered if maybe I ought not to go up there and see about her. On second thought, I figured I couldn't really do anything and that it would only make her more nervous knowing I was so concerned about her. You can't win with a nervous person no matter what you do. Still . . .

Once the news spread through the prayer chain, every last one of the W.W.s called me. Those women get confused real easy, especially when word is passed from one to another of them. Some of them thought it was Beatrice that got robbed. By the time I straightened them out, answered their questions, and repeated the story over and over, I was wore out. "Get off the phone," I would tell them. "Beatrice might be calling me."

But she didn't.

That night I tumbled and tossed and didn't get a wink of sleep. So before daylight I just got up and made the coffee. The Psalms is supposed to comfort a body, so I read a few of them, but there was nothing that jumped out at me. When it got light, I walked down to the garden in my bathrobe, although I'm usually dressed by daylight.

The garden was about burnt up, it was so dry. I couldn't afford to water it enough; my bill was sky-high. I'd shoot just enough water on it to keep stuff alive, but that's not the way to treat a garden.

As I sat there looking at my poor, sorry garden, I thought about Elijah. I needed to go down and see him, but I didn't want to leave the phone in case Beatrice called. I knew Elijah wouldn't never have another mule, and I got to thinking maybe he could use a tiller. It was too soon to ask him, of course, hurt as he was, but I figured it wouldn't do no harm for me to check the ads and take a look-see at yard sales. People buy them things, use them once or twice, and never roll them out again. Next time they clean out the garage, they have a sale, and you can get that tiller at a giveaway price.

I walked back in the house, but I couldn't get nothing done. I wasn't hungry, so I went on the porch and fed the birds. Since there was no water in the birdbath, I filled it up before I went back inside.

I was tired, and seeing as I was not going to get anything done, I picked up my Bible and sat down to read a while. I read three or four chapters, but it was no use; I couldn't have told you one thing I read. I closed my eyes and just asked the Lord to forgive me and do whatever he would for Beatrice.

Knowing I was expecting a call from Beatrice, the W.W.s left off calling me for one day, which has got to be a record. In a way, I wouldn't have minded if one of them had called. There was nothing on TV and I was too lazy to cook. I was just rattling around in the house, so I picked up the phone and called Thelma to remind her to check on Maude's grave.

"We've already checked," she told me. "So far there's been no sign of grave robbers. Has Beatrice called?"

"Not yet," I said and hung up. I knew Thelma was disappointed not to have any further news to spread around.

The phone didn't ring until after six o'clock. When it did, it made me jump, and my heart started beating fast. It was Beatrice.

"Esmeralda, they've caught two suspects, but they weren't wearing masks, so they're probably not the real robbers."

"What do you mean? They wouldn't be wearing masks except when they're holding up a store."

"Don't worry me with details, Esmeralda. I'm too nervous to live, much less think straight. I've broke out in a rash that is itching me to death. I've got more on me than a body can take, what with murderers on the loose and them two upstairs. Last night he left, slammed the door on his way out, stomped down the stairs, and left her bawling upstairs. I could hear her on the phone to her mama. He don't come home until the wee hours. I can't put up with much more of this. I tell you, Esmeralda, I have about had it. I might just as well give up this job, move back to Live Oaks, and get set up in the county home."

"Now, Beatrice, you're overreacting. Calm down. Those gunmen are behind bars, and as for the situation upstairs, there is no reason why that has to go on forever. Just give me a little time, and I'll think of something. Right now, we got to take care of that itch."

The phone cord was all kinked up again, but this was no time to try to unkink it. She was historical. "They may be behind bars, but you know our court system lets criminals go scot-free. Our jails have got swinging doors! I'm about to have a nervous breakdown, Esmeralda. I can't go on like this."

"Yes, you can. Now get hold of yourself!"

"Get hold of myself? How can I? I come to work, and first thing happens is that termite man. He gets his coffee, then comes up to the counter and hangs around—

reads the warning on the cig pack, puts it down, says he don't smoke, as if that mattered to me. Told me his name, Carl something-or-other, as if I wanted to know. Then he starts with the questions: Do I like to go to picture shows? Do I like to bowl? All he gets out of me is a grunt, and I keep so busy behind the counter that I do everything twice that can be done."

She was running on at the mouth like a floodgate let loose. I had to stop her somehow.

"Beatrice, have you forgot what I told you when this thing first happened?"

"What about?"

"About the Lord protecting you."

"No, I have not forgot, but I don't understand why I should fear God. He's the onliest one I am not afraid of."

Oh, my, I thought. *How in the world can I ever get through to her on that?* I took a deep breath. "Beatrice, to fear God don't mean what you think. When you are not so nervous and we can sit down and talk about that, I'll try to explain it. It'll take a lot of time for me to get through to you, but I think I can do it."

"What about the angels? Do you think when I'm in that store, there's a flock of angels around me?"

That made me squirm a bit. "Who needs angels," I said, "when we have got Jesus? When angels aren't praising the Lord, all they do is run errands. People who don't know the first thing about Jesus have gone crazy over angels. You have got Jesus. He will never leave you nor forsake you."

It was the best I could do under the circumstances. And it was the truth.

Beatrice heaved a big sigh. "Esmeralda," she said, "I don't mean to complain. I am thankful to the Lord they caught suspects, but this rash is itching me so bad, I am about to go out of my mind."

"Beatrice," I said, "you and I both have been out of our minds for years. Both of us together do not make a whole wit."

She didn't catch that. Anyway, she was in no mood to joke around. "All right, then," I said. "A skin rash is nothing to keep. Don't go to a doctor. He'll put you on nerve pills, and with your low blood, you would never wake up. Instead of scratching yourself raw, splash on plenty of witch hazel, and when you take your bath, put olive oil in the water, then drip-dry when you get out."

"I have not got no olive oil," she said.

"Any kind of cooking oil will have to do. Now as for your nerves, give me a break! The holdup men are behind bars, I have got a plan to solve the problem upstairs, and when you're up to it, I have something to say about the pigtail man that will surprise you. Everything is under control. You got nothing to worry about, so get over it!"

That night I slept like a log, and I hoped she did too. But I doubted she would.

9

Soon after we talked, I got a note from Beatrice. In it, she enclosed a dollar to give to Elijah in memory of Maude, and there were a few scribbled lines. *Tell Elijah I cried when I heard Maude passed. How is he holding up?*

Well, that gave me an excuse to go visit Elijah, as if I ever needed an excuse to do that. When I got to his place, those kids we saw up on the tracks were playing in the branch out in front. Elijah came to the car, and I asked him who those kids were, but he just said they were catching tadpoles. Well, I could see that for myself, but there was no use pressing Elijah. He was not going to say nothing. Maybe he didn't know nothing.

I told him the dollar was from Beatrice and how she cried and all. His bottom lip commenced to trembling, and he couldn't say nothing. He'd known Beatrice since she was a little kid.

He took his time folding that dollar bill so it would fit in the bib pocket of his overalls. Then he cleared his throat and asked me to tell Beatrice how much obliged he was.

I didn't tell Elijah about the robbery. You do not tell a grieving man any bad news. But I did let him know the W.W.s were taking turns checking on Maude's grave and would keep that up as long as it seemed necessary. I made a mental note to check on the grave myself.

"I'm sorry the Lord didn't answer our prayers about Maude," I said. "I reckon she just died of old age."

"I reckon," he said, quiet like, so I didn't know if he agreed about that or not.

I racked my brain for something more to say, but there was nothing going on that was very uplifting. Then it slipped out. "Pastor Osborne has been taking a lot of brickbats here lately."

Elijah didn't say anything, and that quiet just got deeper, the way it does when he's rolling something around in his mind.

Well, there was nothing more to be said about that, so I climbed out of the car and got the box out of the backseat.

"I brought you some jars of corn, beans, okra, and the like," I told him. He thanked me and took the box. We went inside his little dark cook room, and I set the jars on the table. He keeps that cook room cleaner than I keep my kitchen.

We went back outside where it was cooler, and Elijah pointed me to a rickety chair under the shade of the china-berry tree. Once I was sat down, he parked himself on a bench propped against the tree. I remembered that bench being up at a school bus stop, all the slats broke out. I'd wondered what had happened to it. Elijah must've dragged it home and fixed it up.

I wanted to speak to him about a tiller and thought I'd warm up to the subject.

"Do you think my garden will make?"

He looked off toward the children. "It won't do much if we don't get rain."

"That's what I figger."

We sat there quiet, enjoying a little breeze that whispered in the tree leaves. A June bug was buzzing somewhere. "Any chance we'll get some rain?"

Rubbing his head with the knuckles of his knobby old hand, he said, "Not anytime soon, 'less the Lord takes a notion to give us some."

The children were squealing and running barefoot, splashing in the water. As we watched them, I figured Elijah knew more about them than he was telling me, and if he did, I needn't to worry. He would see that no harm came to them.

I gave up on talking about the tiller. Elijah's heart was too heavy. And then, too, I figured I might not be able to find one. Besides, he would need a vehicle to haul it in.

"Elijah, you need anything?" Of course, he wouldn't tell me if he did. "You let me know if I can do anything for you. Need a ride to town?"

"No'm."

Well, I had to go, so I stood up. I was about to get back in the Chevy when he called to me. "Miz Esmeralda, if you get a chance, ask your preacher to pray for us some rain."

I stopped dead in my tracks and looked back at him. I knew exactly what he was up to. He wanted me to ask that so the preacher would know he had no hard feelings about Maude, and also, more important than anything, that he still believed in Pastor Osborne's prayers.

On the way home I kept thinking about Elijah asking me to do that. I don't know one white man in Live Oaks who would've picked up on the preacher's feelings and figured out a way to encourage him. It takes a long life of living, living beset with put-downs and downright meanness, to spot the same trouble in another man.

I say Elijah's wisdom goes beyond just knowing how that kind of trouble feels—he knows how to do something about it. I decided that hard knocks alone don't give him that gift; Elijah's wisdom comes from above.

I couldn't wait to get home and call Pastor Osborne. I got him on the first ring.

After I got that done, the next day I made it a point to get back in touch with Beatrice. If she was in a better frame of mind, I had something to tell her that would require my best powers of persuasion. Since she was off work on Friday, I put in the call as soon as I thought she would be up. I knew my phone bill was going to look like the national debt if I kept this up much longer, but I didn't know what that girl would do without me.

As it turned out, I caught her just as she rolled out. Of course, she hadn't slept much because of the noise upstairs, but I didn't jump on that right away. We shot the breeze a few minutes, and then I got down to business.

"Beatrice," I said, "now you listen to me. I have got a foolproof strategy that will take care of the problem you've got with the neighbors. Take them something to eat."

"What!" She sounded like she was going to come through the receiver.

"You heard me. Like as not, the wife can't cook, so a dish of something will be a treat they can't turn down."

"You must be kidding!"

"No, I am not. Make your specialty, that lemon meringue pie. Pile it up high. As soon as they come home from work, march yourself up them steps and knock on the door. Whichever one comes to the door, introduce yourself. If they don't invite you in, give them the pie anyway and suggest in a nice way that they can return the plate when it's convenient. If they ask you to come inside, do. Visit with them a little while, then ask them to come visit you sometime."

"You must be out of your mind!"

"I am, but so are you, remember?"

"Esmeralda, there is no way in the world I can do that. They come in fighting like the gingham dog and the calico cat! They like as not throw that pie right back in my face."

"Have you not had a pie throwed in your face before? You will live, I guarantee."

"No. There is no way in the world I could do that."

I got very quiet, and I stayed that way a full minute, although every second was costing me.

"Esmeralda? Esmeralda, are you there?"

Before she started clicking the phone and cut us off, I answered. "I'm here."

"Well, why don't you say something?"

"I did."

"I know, but—"

"Beatrice, what I've suggested is no big thing. One time not long ago, you said you wished there was something you could do for the Lord. I don't look at it that way, because I try to do everything for the Lord, but if that's your way of thinking, I won't question it. Well, now, here is something you can do for the Lord, and you're balking like a mule."

"To do for the Lord?" she repeated, and I knew I had scored a bull's-eye.

"That's right. Jesus said, 'Love your neighbor.' Are those two upstairs your neighbors or are they not?"

"Oh, Esmeralda, I wish you wouldn't put it thataway."

I sighed loud enough for her to hear. "Do as you like, Beatrice. If you can't do a little thing like that for Jesus, I don't know what to make of you. I got to hang up. This is costing me an arm and a leg."

That's the way you had to handle Beatrice sometimes—shame her. That poor girl was so timid and so scared, and I knew it would be very hard for her, but it was the right thing to do. I couldn't wait to hear how it turned out. I had a bigger bombshell to land on her once she got over this one.

That night after supper, I went out on the porch, feeling good about what I had accomplished, and I sat on the glider for a while, enjoying myself. The fireflies were as thick as ever I'd seen them. Reminded me how we children used to catch fireflies and put 'em in a fruit jar to watch 'em light up. All the neighborhood kids would gather outside of an evening and have the most fun playing in the yard—games like Giant Step and so forth. We'd wind up under the streetlight on the corner, telling ghost stories and getting so scared we had to have somebody go with us when we ran home.

Sitting on the glider is where I do my best praying and thinking. I had a lot of both to do that night, and the time slipped up on me. I was about ready to get up and go inside when I saw a woman coming down the street. I didn't see her until she came under the streetlight, but that's when she stopped. I figured she needed to hitch up her pantyhose or something, but she didn't bend over or nothing. It was curious she would stop like that. I craned my neck, trying to see if she was anybody I knew—and I knew nearly every woman in Live Oaks. Well, as I came to think on it, I didn't know one who would be out that late at night by theirselves.

I was real puzzled. She began walking a few steps one way, turned around, and walked a few steps the other way. *She must be lost,* I thought. Then she just stood there. A few cars went by on the street, and when the first one passed, I could see in the headlights that this woman was not dressed right. She didn't have on enough clothes to hide her nakedness!

Well, I don't have to be hit over the head with a sledgehammer to know a thing when I see it. That woman was nothing but a streetwalker!

After discovering that fact, I couldn't go to bed. I watched her hour after hour as she plied her trade, but one car after another whizzed past her. Business was not good, which was a credit to the community.

When she finally gave up and disappeared into the darkness at four o'clock in the morning, I got up, thoroughly disgusted, and went to bed.

As wide awake as the owls hooting in the trees, I lay there thinking what I must do. I decided I would keep this to myself and see how it went. Let one word slip out that there was a prostitute in town and every woman in Live Oaks would lock up every husband or boyfriend they had got. Let them find out for theirselves; I for one was not going to tell a single soul, not even Beatrice, who lived a hundred miles away.

I did tell the Lord, though.

Saturday night, I kept watch again. At about midnight, a white truck slowed down, went around the block, and came back. I knew business was picking up. Whoever it was stopped and looked like he was talking to her through the window. Then the door opened, she got in, and they went on down the street. The truck never came back.

It made my heart heavy knowing that such was going on right under my nose, so it was a relief to get up Sunday morning and go to the house of the Lord. In class I had nothing to say to the W.W.s, and I could tell that made them curious, but I had too much on my mind to bother about them. I hardly heard a word Thelma was teaching.

In the worship service, during the long prayer, Pastor Osborne prayed for rain—not just showers, but for real rain such as we needed, the slow, steady kind that lasts until the ground gets good and soaked. In my heart I said, *Thank you, Jesus.*

Well, brother, if I had known what the fallout would be, I never would've asked Pastor Osborne to pray for rain! After church, people didn't hightail it to the all-you-can-eat restaurant but stood around outside, not saying much. But what they did say, they said in a shifty kind of way.

"What in the world is going on?" I asked, but nobody said nothing. Then some little kid piped up, "Preacher Bob prayed for rain."

"Well, what's wrong with that? We shore need it!"

Clara whispered in my ear but loud enough for others to hear, "Well, what if it don't rain?"

"So what? When you've prayed, have you never had the Lord say no? Mercy me, I have!"

She twisted those thin lips the way she does when she feels she's way ahead. "It's the children, Esmeralda. How do you explain to little children that the Lord don't answer their preacher's prayers? What are they going to think of the Lord, much less Preacher Bob?"

"The Lord can take care of himself," I snapped. But I wasn't so sure the pastor could, not with all those vultures perched to gobble him up alive.

Mabel Elmwood whispered something in her husband's ear, he nodded, and then she called for everyone's attention. "Our senior elder has something to say." She looked up at him like he was Moses come down from Mount Sinai.

Roger Elmwood cleared his throat, and in that politician's voice of his, he said, "Friends, it is the better part of wisdom to pray for rain only in the privacy of one's own closet. That way we don't run into questions when it don't rain. We have a responsibility to those who are weak in the faith, for children and young people who are not yet mature Christians, to avoid creating a problem that could possibly turn them away from the Lord."

Every one of those fainthearted, pious members standing around either said amen or expressed their agreement by nodding their heads up and down.

I, for one, came right back at him. "Well," I said, "I think it is the better part of faith to pray for rain in public and bring your umbrella! Splurgeon says faith honors Christ and Christ honors faith."

Well, then Thelma just had to put her two cents in. "The weather report on Channel 9 says there won't be rain until next month, if then."

"Have they not been wrong more times than they have been right?" I asked. "I tell you, no weatherman has got God in his pocket. The Lord will do what he wants to do without asking them!"

I got a lot of looks that said "You poor thing" as the crowd took off for the restaurant.

Every day I looked for rain, but it didn't come. And every day the talk about it got bolder. The talk went on over the telephone, in stores, down at the washerette, the barbershop, and the beauty parlor—everywhere I went. The weather just got hotter and drier, not a cloud in the sky. The only reason the W.W.s didn't let me in on their grapevine was that they didn't want to be caught short if it did rain. Hedging their bets, don't you know. But by Friday it still had not rained, and they couldn't stand it no longer. Two of them came up the walk, and since they'd waited a long time to throw in my face about the preacher praying for Maude and getting no answer, I figured this was the time they would bring it up.

I served them ice tea on the porch. Clara didn't say much; she seemed nervous and mumbled something about how we all of us believe in prayer. Still hedging her bets.

Mabel Elmwood, who is usually quiet until everybody else has had their say and she can tell which way the wind is blowing before she puts in her two cents, had no hang-up about speaking out.

"I feel so sorry for Roger," she began in her mealy-mouth way. "He says that praying for Maude posed a real problem for the elders, who could not support Pastor Bob's view. Fortunately, Maude died, making it plain to see that it is not right to pray for animals. Roger says Preacher Bob should've learned his lesson then and been more careful about what he prayed for in public."

"She's talking about rain," Clara said, as if I didn't know.

"Yes, praying for rain is a risky thing to do," Mabel continued. "It shows poor judgment on the preacher's part. You see, Roger says Preacher Bob does not have to deal with the questions, it's the elders. As the spiritual leaders, they are the ones who have to answer all the questions this kind of thing raises."

Clara reached over and put a pillow behind Mabel's back. "Thank you," Mabel said. "This old glider is uncomfortable."

I could have crowned her!

"Now what was I saying? Oh yes. Preacher Bob should not have been so sure of himself to pray publicly for rain after the experience of the mule."

I could not stand another word. "Pastor Osborne is not sure of himself, he is sure of God, which is more than I can say for most of them elders."

Well, she brushed me off like I was some kind of historical female. "The elders are thinking about bringing Preacher Bob in for counseling."

I tell you what, I was about to blow a gasket. The nerve of them people! What them two wanted was a rise out of me so they could go back and tell everybody what I said and the way I acted. Well, I said nothing, and when they saw I was not going to play their little game, they got themselves up and left.

After them two went home, I was so mad I lay across the bed and beat the pillow with my fists. I had not had a spell like that since before Bud died. It was Friday, and not one drop of rain had fallen. I couldn't bear to think of that poor man getting up in the pulpit Sunday morning with all those self-righteous, backbiting hypocrites looking up at him. "Lord," I said, trying not to be mad, "whyn't you do the preacher and me one big favor and send us a gully washer before Sunday?"

Upon my word, I am telling you the gospel truth—twenty-five minutes later, if you go by my bedroom clock, I heard a rumble. At first I thought it was a plane flying overhead. But the rumbling come closer, and then right over my house there was a big boom. I could not believe my ears! I jumped up and went out on the porch. That cloud was as black as midnight! Sheet lightning was flashing all around, and the wind was picking up. "Lord, is this what I hope it is?" I asked.

Sure enough, in a few minutes, big drops were peppering down. The thunder was booming, and the rain was coming fast. The smell of it was delicious! I watched it coming down the street, washing everything in its path, the runoff flooding alongside the curbs, rushing down the drains. I was so happy I could've run outside in that rain buck naked!

10

It rained all Friday night, a slow steady rain. Saturday morning a drizzle set in, but in the afternoon the sun came out long enough for me to take a look at the garden. It did my heart good to see puddles running down between the rows. My tomatoes, kind of beat down by the rain, looked like they didn't know what to make of it. But they popped right back up and started growing. So did the weeds. Weeds are like sins—they grow faster than the good stuff.

By the time I got back in the house, it was coming down again. It rained off and on all Saturday night, but it didn't keep that woman from walking the street below my house. I watched her a little while, but it was such a good night for sleeping, I decided to go to bed. I made up my mind that when the weather let up and I could hide in the bushes, I was going to get the license number of that white truck if he picked her up again.

By Sunday morning it had quit raining, except for drops falling off the trees. A lot of people didn't show up for church, but those that did—well, sheep never looked so sheepish.

Monday morning I got a note from Beatrice telling me she had taken the pie upstairs.

I went upstairs with that pie like you told me to. My knees were knocking even though he was not yelling and she was not crying. When they let me in, I asked them what they fight about and he laughed and said, "Any little thing comes up," and she laughed too. I was so nerviss I didn't stay long but I did remember to invite them to come to see me sometime and they both started talking about how busy they were. Esmeralda, I really don't think I can handle them visiting me but I asked them to bring my plate back so I guess one of them will have to come downstairs.

They did not fight last night. I fell asleep listening to them up there laughing.

Esmeralda, I did this for Jesus. I hope you are satisfied.

I was. I was pleased as punch. She was making a good start, and I felt I could drop the other bombshell on her, so I wrote her right back. I cut it short about the rain and all, then wrote:

Beatrice, I have got the letter you wrote a while back about that pigtail man. It's right here on my lap. You say in your letter he comes in the store every day and he asked if you liked to go to the picture show and if you liked to bowl.

Have you got no sense? That man is showing interest in you. Before you have a dying duck fit, give it some thought. I have been asking the Lord for some time to give you a man friend—not a husband, just a man friend. When we pray we have got to look for an answer, so that is what I'm asking you to do.

From what you say, this Carl sounds like he is on in years. Don't let that turn you off. You and I are not spring chickens running around with roosters. At your age you can't expect to get a man who has not been pre-owned even if now he is not owned lock, stock, and barrel. A widderwer is your best bet. Next time Carl comes in the store, you take a good look at him and write me what you find out.

I was surprised Beatrice didn't call me right up after she got my letter. After two or three days I was beginning to wonder if Carl had quit coming in the store. I hoped she was just too busy. One good thing about Beatrice is she never gets mad at me, and I must admit I have been pretty hard on her at times.

There's a hedge runs around my place, and before that streetwalker put in her nightly appearance, I took a little stool out there and positioned myself behind the hedge where I could get a close enough view to read any license plate that came along. I had my pencil and pad resting on my knee, and at about ten o'clock, there she was. Well, I tell you, I was so close I could nearly see the whites of her eyes! Her skirt was short, and them skinny legs were wobbling on heels as high as ever I'd seen. There was something draped around her shoulders like a scarf, and it looked like that was all she had on. Mercy me, I had seen such women on TV, but seeing one live was something I could do without.

She was not an older woman. Most of them aren't old, I'm told, but she looked old in the face. And she was twitching like a scairt rabbit. Under any other circumstances, I would've felt sorry for her. I tell you the truth, that woman was so thin that when she was on the other side of the lamppost, there wasn't enough of her showing for me to see! That lifestyle sure takes its toll.

Well, I'll tell you what, that little old stool is not the most comfortable thing to sit on, and as the night stretched on, I got leg cramps to beat the band and a backache to break all records. As cars were few and far between and none of them stopped, I was beginning to think my misery was all for naught.

Even the streetwalker got tired and leaned up against the lamppost. I would've gone back inside, but I couldn't without her seeing me. I was stuck right there on that stool until she made up her mind to leave. Finally, she sat down on the curb, but still she didn't go home. She must've been desperate, to hang on like she did.

Along about three o'clock, I heard a vehicle turn the corner, and when it got in sight, I saw it was a white pickup. The driver knew right where he was headed and hardly slowed down before he stopped at the streetlight. Without a word spoken, she hopped in, and in my disgust, I almost forgot what my mission was. Fortunately, it was an easy number and a South Carolina plate. I didn't even have to write it down.

I was excited about getting the evidence, and I didn't sleep much. The next morning I was at the sheriff's office by eight o'clock. As usual, Sheriff Thigpen was the only one in the office, and he was reading the newspaper.

"Good morning, Esmeralda. What can I do for you?"

"I got a license number I want you to look up."

"I'd be glad to do that for you." He rolled his chair over to the computer. "Gimme the number."

"It's South Carolina, 409 ARK."

The sheriff stopped short, his mouth dropped, and he shot me a look I'll never forget. "What you want that number for?"

"Nothing important. Just curious."

"Curious?" He stared at me. "It don't have nothing to do with burying that mule, does it?"

"No, nothing about the mule. Why do you ask?"

He shifted his chair back to the desk. "Well, Esmeralda, this is my son's number. If he's in any kind of trouble . . ."

I had to think fast. "Oh, Sheriff, don't you think you'd be the first to know if Horace was in trouble?"

"Well, then, what is it brings you down here at eight o'clock in the morning, wanting to know my son's license plate number?"

I tell you, the man was getting downright insistent. "Well, if you must know . . ." Then it came to me. "Sheriff, I'm planning on buying Elijah a tiller, but I have got to find something for him to haul it around town in. I was just hoping the owner of that old white pickup would be willing to sell. If the price is right, I might be able to raise the money to buy it."

Sheriff Thigpen relaxed. "Oh, I see." He laughed a little. "You had me worried there for a minute. When Horace buried the mule for you, he come home and told me that you and them Willing Workers is something to be reckoned with. You want me to call him?"

"No, that's all right," I said, heading for the door. "I'll take care of it later."

Boy, was I glad to get out of there! My conscience was beating up on me about lying like that, and I know I had to find a tiller so I wouldn't be outright lying for long.

When I got back home, the mail had already come. Along with a bill, there was a note from Beatrice.

I read it as I was walking back to the house, skipping down to the part where she wrote:

Esmeralda, you must be out of your mind. There is no way in this wide world I can believe that man Carl has taken a fancy to me. *Besides, I am not the least bit interested in any man.*

But I done what you asked me to. I looked him over good this morning. Looks like he shaves every day and he wears round glasses with a ribbon holding them on. No long nose or nothing and although he crawls around under houses looking for bugs he is clean. Of course, that pigtail sticking out from underneath his baseball cap is most likely not clean. I hate that thing. He don't ever take off that cap. Chances are he is bald on top. If he has a potbelly he keeps it covered under his jacket. On second thought, he does not wear a jacket so he must not have a potbelly. If he didn't have that pigtail he would be an all right looking man but looks is not everything. He must not be married, he don't wear a wedding ring. What more do you want to know?

I felt good about that letter. Given enough time to collect my thoughts, I would write her a letter and see if maybe we could get something going there.

My phone was ringing. I picked it up, wondering if it was Beatrice.

"Miss Esmeralda?" It was a man's voice.

"That's right."

"This is Horace Thigpen. We have got to talk." He didn't wait for me to say anything. "I'll be up to your house in five minutes."

11

In a few minutes I heard the squeal of tires as that truck turned the corner. Horace Thigpen wheeled up my driveway so fast he clipped my blue hydrangea. I met him on the porch.

He was white as hoarfrost froze solid. "Miss Esmeralda, I want to know how you got my license number and why."

"Well, Horace, I see you driving all over town." I was stalling, trying to come up with an answer that wouldn't give me away. "I could've got it in the parking lot down at the sheriff's office." As soon as I said it, I knew he could see right through me.

"What do you mean you 'could have'? You know good and well where you got it!"

My heart was thumping. "Oh, I do, do I? Horace Thigpen, I am a busy woman, and with all I got to do, there's no reason under the sun why I should clutter my mind with details such as that."

He parked himself on the glider. "Miss Esmeralda, I'm sitting right here until you tell me the truth. I believe you hid in them bushes down there next to the street and got my license number in the dead of night."

Well, I saw no use in denying it. "Horace, I didn't know it was your truck."

"You do now!"

I was afraid to open my mouth. When Horace saw I wasn't going to volunteer anything more, he stormed out at me. "What business is it of yours how I spend my time, where I go, what I do? You're just a nosy woman out to cause trouble for other people. And you call yourself a Christian! Exactly what did you plan to do once you got my number?"

"I don't know. I didn't have a plan exactly, but I'll tell you right now, we don't need such as that going on in Live Oaks."

He snorted. "You don't live in the real world, Esmeralda. You and them religious pokes have got nothing better to do than take away the rights of people like me. A man has got a right to his own kind of pleasure if it don't hurt nobody else. What harm is it to you?"

"Do you want a glass of tea?"

"No, I do not want a glass of tea!" He stood up to look out the porch. "I guess you've spread this around to all your busybody friends."

"No, Horace, I haven't. I haven't told a single soul." I sat down on the other end of the glider, hoping that might help cool him down, but he kept on ranting.

"That cock-and-bull story about wanting to buy my truck—what makes you think my truck is for sale?" He didn't expect an answer, obviously, because he kept right on going. "That was just an excuse you give my daddy, but I tell you, Esmeralda, you better not tell him anything different. And I better not hear you've told anybody else how you got my number. If I hear one word of this, it is just possible Elijah's shack will burn to the ground, with him in it."

"What? Are you threatening me? How dare you!"

"You heard me. Elijah has got no business using kerosene lamps in that shack. They explode easy. Besides, any puff of wind can turn one over. Nobody would ever believe a fire at his place was anything more than an accident. Do you get my drift?"

"Get off my porch, Horace Thigpen. Get off right this minute!"

He smirked. "I see you got my drift."

I wanted to throw him down the steps, but he took them two at a time and jumped in his truck. I yelled after him, "Horace Thigpen, be sure your sin will find you out!"

As he backed down the driveway, I could see that he was grinning.

I turned, went back in the house, and slammed the screen door. I was so mad I was talking to myself out loud. When I'm mad like that, work is the only thing helps get it out of my system. I got the hoe and headed for the garden.

Chopping weeds, I went over that conversation a thousand times. I tried to think of what I might've said different so as not to show my hand, but chances were he knew the truth anyway and nothing I said would've fooled him.

It did unsettle me to be called nosy. And also the things he said about Christians. Were we a bunch of busybodies? Well, I didn't know about that. Maybe we were.

Maybe I was.

At the end of a row, I leaned on the hoe a long time, wondering about that. Finally, I went back to chopping and muttered, "Lord, let me know what you think."

It was Wednesday, and by suppertime I had to stop and get ready for a missions meeting at church. I took my bath, washed my hair, rolled it up, and watched the news while I ironed my red blouse.

After the news went off, I unplugged the iron, folded up the board, and cleaned my teeth. After getting dressed, I brushed out my hair and sprayed it good. When I was powdering my face, I studied what I was seeing in the mirror. "Esmeralda," I said to myself, "you are one old fool. Do you think Jesus would hide in the bushes to get the goods on somebody?" Of course, he wouldn't have to. But be that as it may, like as not he would wait his time and, given the opportunity, love that whoremonger until that sorry person gave up and repented.

I did not feel good about myself.

At the church, as I was climbing out of my Chevy, I could hear the band instruments getting tuned up. What a racket! I knew that if I could hear it out in the parking lot, it would be louder still inside. Much as that would bug me, I was determined not to say one word about it.

The missions group was meeting in the W.W.s' classroom across the hall from where Boris's practice session was going on. The women were not happy about giving up the fellowship hall for the young people, and the noise threatening to drown out our meeting did not help matters. Clara, whose granddaughter had become a star performer in the youth group, was trying to stay on top of the situation, but already there was an undercurrent of comments being passed around. I knew Clara would try to keep the lid on any criticism about Boris's music program, but she might just as well try to put a lid on a volcano determined to erupt. Standing behind the podium, she held on to it like she needed support and commenced the meeting on time.

We had prayer and the usual stuff before Clara started reading a letter from missionaries. Trembling like she was, the paper in her hands rattled and her voice got screechy as it rose above the racket coming from across the hall.

While reading at the top of her lungs, the tune-ups stopped, and she was left hollering so loud you could hear her downtown. I had a hard time keeping a straight face.

Clara quieted down and resumed reading just as the youth choir began rehearsing. Naturally, everybody tuned out Clara to listen to the singing. Seeing she had lost them, Clara stopped reading the letter and turned to the business of raising money for AIDS orphans. The women did not reach for their pocketbooks, because they weren't listening to her. Clara was frantic, wide-eyed and screaming to be heard, straining her neck, stretching it so long she could've passed for an ostrich.

It's a good thing she was screaming real loud, because the band started up again. The trumpets and the trombones were not getting along together, so Boris would stop them and then get them started again, only to stop them a second and third time. To keep up with this, Clara's voice went up and down like a yo-yo. With the sudden stops, she would be caught yelling so loud the kids could hear her in the fellowship hall. About the time she brought down the volume, the band would start up again. That woman has got one shrill voice.

Finally, the band calmed down and a violin took over. The look on Clara's face was something to behold. From screaming, she switched to beaming. Wiping perspiration from her forehead, she put her neck back in place and for once shut up. In the middle of whatever her granddaughter was playing, the music stopped and we heard the girl say, "I popped a string." That was the end of her solo, and in two minutes the full force of horns was blasting again, the sound bouncing off the walls, down the hall, out the windows.

That's when the stack blew, and the criticisms began to pelt down on Boris Krantz. "I've had about enough of that!" Thelma said, her voice loud and clear above the noise.

The high-sounding horns and the big, booming drums reverberating all around did not let up, and Mabel clapped her hands over her ears. "Brass horns and drums have got no place in church!"

Like that little boy with his finger in the dike, Clara tried to stop the gushing of hot words. "Oh, ladies, let's not criticize," she yelled in that trumpet swan voice of hers. "Music has done wonders for my granddaughter."

I believe I'm the only one heard Clara, because the other women were all talking at once.

"You call that music?" someone hooted.

"Whatever it is, it is outrageous!"

"Why, you could dance by what they were singing just minutes ago."

"They practically do dance—swing their hips with the rhythm, snap their fingers, and so on."

The sparks were flying, and a prairie fire couldn't spread no faster.

"Ladies! Ladies!" Clara screeched. "We must get back to the program. Pleeeze!"

But there was no reining them in—they were off to the races. "Ain't it enough that Boris is bringing that homeless man to church? Why, that man is no doubt a drug addict."

"Or running from the law."

"Could be a gangster, a murderer, or who knows what!"

"Most likely, he's a pedophile coming to church to prey on our young people."

Thelma leaned straight forward in her chair. "I know from my experience up North that street people bring vermin into the rescue missions. What will the deacons do when vermin gets in and piles up in the corner of a pew?"

I, for one, didn't know who Vermin was, but I say, whoever is brought to church is a good thing. I didn't open my mouth, however.

In that pious way of hers, Mabel Elmwood pursed her lips and informed us, "I like the old hymns. They have got a message." Then she kind of giggled. "Roger says these songs the young people sing is nothing but a 'seven eleven'—seven words sung eleven times."

If that was supposed to be funny, I didn't get it.

A loud drumroll was knocking my hearing aid out of commission. When the noise finally stopped, Thelma stood up. "If you ask me, ladies, it is high time the deacons put Boris Krantz on notice that he has got to clean up his act!"

Clara, wringing her hands and about to cry, sputtered, "Please, ladies, pleeeze!"

I should've nipped the thing in the bud, but now that the pot was boiling over, I took charge. I stood up, and they all put their mouths on hold for a minute to look at me. I deliberately took my time, knowing it would make them more curious. I laid my pocketbook on the chair, straightened my skirt, and with my Bible under my arm, marched up front. Motioning Clara aside, I took over the podium, waited for her to sit down, then laid my Bible open on the speaker's stand. The music had stopped, and everything was so quiet you could've heard a pin drop.

First, I asked if they had forgot the jazzy choruses we used to sing when we were young. Clara's head was going up and down like one of them stuffed puppies in the back window of a car.

"Half them choruses had no Christian message to speak of," I told them, "and if they did, it went right out the window. Even back then, I wondered why we were climbing Jacob's Ladder, and as for 'Give Me Oil in My Lamp,' I didn't see no need of that since we all had electricity. The most we did was sing our hearts out and make a joyful noise, thinking it was unto the Lord."

"That's right," Clara said, her voice so high that she sounded historical. "Go on, Esmeralda, go on."

I flipped the pages of my Bible until I came to the Chronicles and a verse I had marked. "Listen to this: 'And David and all Israel played before God with all their might, and with singing, and with harps, and with psalteries, and with timbrels.'" I looked down over my glasses at them. I didn't have to say a word, because I could see that what I was getting at was soaking in.

Then I continued. "As for brass horns and drums in the church, may I remind you ladies that the Lord uses trumpets so much in the Bible, they must be his favorite instrument? He even lets Gabriel use one. At the sound of the last trumpet, I hope you ladies will not be put off by it being a loud brass instrument and miss the rapture."

They didn't like that one bit and squirmed in their seats, ready to come back at me. But I wasn't through. "May I remind you that King David's psalms are full of clanging cymbals and trumpets? They used anything they could get their hands on, not just harps. Let me read you just one verse from Psalm Ninety-eight." As I turned the pages, I told them, "When you go home, mark it in your Bible. It's verses 8 and 9; no, it's 5 and 6. It reads: 'Sing unto the LORD with the harp; with the harp, and the voice of a psalm. With trumpets and sound of cornet make a joyful noise before the LORD, the King.' Ladies, I have been told David's harp was like a guitar. What do you make of that?"

Nobody challenged me, but I was far from through. They would have to sit tight.

"As for the young people keeping time with their music, swaying a little, well, I don't go for that, because Papa didn't allow us to keep time patting our feet in church. But if you would read your Bible a little more often and a little more carefully, you would know that Miriam and a bunch of women danced with tambourines to celebrate crossing the Red Sea. It was women with women, of course, nothing like couples slow dancing. David danced, too, when he was bringing up the ark. It was only men dancing, of course. Don't you go outta here and say that I said it is all right to dance in church. I don't favor that in the least, but we have got to let the young people enjoy their way of worshiping, even as they let us enjoy our way."

So far, so good. I took a deep breath and dived into the hard part. "Now let me explain something to you." Then I laid it on the line and talked about how music is like language and how our music language is foreign to young people today because they've been brought up on rock and roll, country music, and the like of that. (I was in water over my head trying to think of the different kinds of music they have.)

"Excuse me," Mabel sniffed. "That is worldly music. We are in the world, but we are not of the world."

Before she scored a point, I whipped out my secret weapon, the sword of the Spirit. "Mabel, 'Do unto others as you would have them do unto you.' With all due respect, you have not understood one word I have said here. Much as you and I might like the 'Hallelujah Chorus,' young people don't cotton to that kind of singing; it is not in their language, so to speak. We have been sitting here listening to reports from missionaries in foreign countries. Every one of them missionaries had to learn the language of the people they were sent to win. You should be thankful that you don't have to learn Chinese or this language that's foreign to us, this youth music. We all should shut up and be happy the young people are making music to Jesus. We don't have to like it. I, for one, will not split the church over it."

Just as Clara started clapping, from across the hall came a loud and long drumroll! I wondered if those kids heard my speech and liked it.

Well, that night the women filed outside without asking one question. But Clara hugged me and Thelma murmured, "Thank you, Esmeralda."

When I started out, I didn't know I would win, but I had won hands down! The W.W.s are good Christian women, and once they face the truth, they do what's right. Oh, we have flare-ups now and then, but there's enough of them on the side of the truth to prevent any big eruption.

Boris was safe. Thank the Lord.

As I was coming in the back door of my house, I could hear the phone ringing. It was Beatrice. I had plum forgot about her.

"What is it, Beatrice?"

"It's that man."

"What man?"

"Carl, the one with the pigtail."

"Oh?"

"Esmeralda, he come right out and asked me to go bowling with him. Of course, I flat out refused, but I'm afraid he'll keep pestering me, driving me up the wall."

"He might," I said. "Of course, you need to know more about him. Is he married?"

"No. He don't wear a wedding ring."

"Beatrice, that don't tell you a thing! A man can slip off a wedding ring and not put it back on until he's home again."

"Well, I don't know how to find out if he's married or not, but I tell you frankly, I don't care. I just want him to leave me alone."

"I'll tell you what I'll do. I'll give it some thought and write you a long letter. I'm too tired tonight, but maybe after I get my work done tomorrow, I can sit down and—"

"You needn't to bother. I am not going out with him. Can't you just see me making a fool of myself trying to bowl?"

Yes, I could see that—her throwing the ball and sliding down the alley after it on her backside.

"I told him I couldn't lift one of those bowling balls, and he said we'd use duckpins. What are duckpins?"

"They're smaller balls. You can lift them. Now, Beatrice, don't be too hasty. Remember I told you I've been praying the Lord would bring someone across your path who would be a friend. Let's find out more about Carl before we make up our minds about him."

I don't think she heard me. "One other thing, Esmer-alda. Jim and Sadie brought the plate back and said they liked the pie. They didn't sit down because they were going out to eat. They asked me if I would like to go with them, but I said no, because I already had my meal fixed."

"Well, now, Beatrice. That wasn't so bad after all, was it?"

"No, it wasn't as bad as I thought it would be. Maybe I'll find the energy to make another pie and take it up to them."

"You do that, Beatrice. I need to go to bed. It's been a busy day."

"Okay," she said, and we hung up.

I helped myself to a bowl of butter-pecan ice cream and took it out on the porch to get cooled off before going to bed. What a day it had been! I knew I couldn't stand many more like it.

I had lost interest in the streetwalker, but I did look to see if she was down there. She wasn't.

With the ice cream taken care of, I went inside and got ready for bed. Before turning out the light, I looked down at the streetlight again. The woman still had not shown up.

I slept pretty well, but I got up a couple of times in the night to go to the bathroom. Every time I got up, I checked the streetlight. The woman didn't show up all night long. *Maybe she's found another territory,* I thought.

12

❧

All the next day, I thought about what I should write to Beatrice. When I had it all thought out, I sat down and did it. Here's what I wrote.

Beatrice, about that fellow Carl, forget about the pigtail for a minute. That can wait. What you need to know right up front is: Is this man a Christian? No need to ask him because whether or not he is he will say he is and you won't know anything more than you knew before. The only safe way to find out is to watch the way he lives. Check out his language. "Holy hearts make holy tongues," Splurgeon says. If he can't say nothing good about other people his heart is not right. Does any corrupt communication come out of his mouth like off-color remarks or swear words? If so, drop him like a hot potato.

If he passes those tests, the next thing is: Is he honest? It won't do to just ask him what he would do if he found a wallet with a lot of money in it. To impress you, a liar would give the right answer. You have got to blindside him.

I scratched that last sentence; Beatrice wouldn't know what it meant.

Get him talking about high taxes and ask him what's the best way to get around paying them. Most men can give you a list of smart ways to cheat the government. If he gives a straight answer, something like, "I wouldn't know about that," he is one in a million. Men can't stand admitting they don't know something.

If you determine that he is a Christian, the next thing may not be necessary but with things the way they are nowadays it won't hurt to check it out. You want to make sure he is not a married man. As I told you on the phone, not wearing a wedding ring is no proof whatsoever a man is not married.

The way to tell if a man is married is easy. If he has a decent haircut chances are a wife is back of it. Since Carl has that pigtail you might consider it a pretty good sign he is not married.

If a man is heavy into aftershave and wears a lot of jewelry, he is a man on the prowl, single or married.

A married man is not available at all times. If he has to pick and choose when he can see you it's because he has to find a time when his wife is too busy to notice—she's out of town, at a meeting, or in the hospital. A married man has to touch base at home whenever his wife expects him to so he can't always plan ahead. If he can't stay long, chances are she's on to him and he's afraid she'll catch him.

If he won't take you to public places where he is likely to be seen with you or if he never introduces you to anybody he knows, he is a married man.

A married man does not have sense enough to play hard to get. That's because he is more interested in getting you than in you getting him. He will brag about what he's got, where he's been, and the big plans he has for making his next million. As Splurgeon says, "He that is full of himself is very empty." Such a man will do all the talking to keep you from asking questions. If you do get a word in and ask if he is married, he will lie flat out or tell you some sad story about how his wife left him for his best friend and broke his heart. Don't believe a word of it.

She's probably at home with his kids trying to pay all the bills he has run up.

Another thing. If Carl is in the termite business, don't expect him to have a lot of money to spend. If he does throw money around, look out, he has got something *on the side. No telling what, gambling maybe. Or he is head over heels in debt.*

Find out if he has a neat little lunch in a lunch pail. If he does, he lives with his mama. He is not the marrying kind. Of course, marrying is not something you have in mind either, just friendship, right?

Now to help you get started, since you don't cotton to bowling, next time he asks, turn the tables on him. Invite him to go to church with you. If he is quick to accept and don't ask what church you're going to before he agrees to go, that tells you he is not one of them narrow-minded "we the only church has got the truth" kind of believers. You will feel safe with him in church and besides it will give the women something to talk about. Ha! Ha!

I read that letter over three times before I mailed it.

Over a week went by, and I had not heard a word from Beatrice. I tell you, curiosity was about to kill this cat!

And every night I looked for that prostitute to show up, but she never did. I figured Horace got word to her somehow about my corner being watched and she had staked out a place in another part of town.

I thought a lot about that woman, and I prayed for her, but I just didn't understand why she sold her body when she could be working at an honest job. Standing on a street corner in all kinds of weather, begging men to have their way, well, to me, that would be hell on earth. Not to mention the fact that such a life was sure to lead to hell below. I knew some hookers made good money, but I'd beg before I'd do that.

Another week went by. The only important thing I got done took a giant step of faith. I saw in the want ads that somebody was selling a used tiller. I prayed about it, and since I hadn't been able to find one before, I figured this must be it.

That tiller looked brand new. I couldn't find one thing wrong with it. When I asked the owner why she was selling it, she said her husband had died and she couldn't handle it no more. I was satisfied the tiller was a good buy, so I paid down on it. The woman said she'd keep it in her garage and give me thirty days to come up with the rest of the money. Well, I'd have to ask the Lord for that.

Paying for the tiller was the easy part; finding some kind of vehicle to haul it in was the hard thing. If worse came to worse, poor Elijah would have to make a wagon he could pull himself. I hated to think we might come to that.

The rest of the week all I did was stake tomatoes, wash the car, scrub the front porch, and cut the grass. Oh yes, I peeled and canned a bushel of peaches, made a couple of jars of peach pickle, and took some to Mrs. Purdy.

Little did I know the Lord was giving me a week's rest for what lay ahead. If I had known before what the Lord had in mind for me to do, I might've gone AWOL.

13

At the crack of dawn, somebody was knocking on my back door. I opened it, and there stood Elijah!

"Elijah! What in the world? Come inside, come in here."

He took off his cap and came in the kitchen.

"You walk all the way up here, or did somebody bring you?"

"No'm, I walked."

I poured him a cup of coffee and put in some sugar and milk. He liked plenty of sugar and milk. "I'll fix you some breakfast."

"No'm. We ain't got time for that."

I was holding the frying pan in my hand and looking at him, waiting for him to tell me what was up. "What's the matter, Elijah?"

"Missy, there's something you got to help me with."

He didn't touch the coffee.

"What is it?"

"You'll see. We got to go now."

I put the frying pan away, took off my apron, and got my keys. "Where we going?"

"To my place."

We got in the Chevy. I cranked her up, and we rolled down the driveway. I knew this was some kind of emergency, but when Elijah said, "We got to hurry," I got downright alarmed. It had never been his nature to hurry. Had his house caught on fire? Was one of those children plays around his place hurt?

At that early hour, there was nobody much on the road. Although I am not one to break the speed limit, I broke it that morning. There is a straightaway beyond town, and I gunned it—that Chevy was wide open. Elijah propped both his hands on the dash, bracing for the curve up ahead. As we rounded the bend, tires squealing, Elijah said, "Slow down." I thought he was just scared, but as we approached what looked to be somebody's lane, he said, "See that road up a ways? Turn in there."

I slowed down. "Aren't we going to your place?"

He just grunted.

It wasn't much of a road, only two good ruts. It looked to be the same road Clara took by mistake the day we brought stew beef and rice to Elijah. I remembered now how we rocked along in them ruts until we landed alongside the railroad trestle above Elijah's place. That's where we first saw those little children.

"Something happened to them kids?" I asked Elijah.

He shook his head.

In a few minutes we pulled up alongside the siding with the boxcar on it. "Stop right here, Missy," Elijah said, so I did. Those three children were all sitting in the open door of the boxcar, eating Vienna sausage out of the can. As soon as they saw Elijah, they scrambled down and came running to the car. Elijah got out and picked up the little girl. By the time I got out the car, the boys had wrapped their arms around his legs and didn't look like they would let go anytime soon. Elijah looked back at me and motioned with his head.

I followed him to the boxcar. He put down the little girl and disengaged himself from the boys. "She's in here," he said.

"She?"

Elijah grabbed hold of the side of the door opening, swung up, and reached a hand down to me. The boxcar was dark, and I couldn't see nothing for a minute or two. Then I made out what looked like a pile of rags in the corner.

"This lady is real sick, Missy. I'm scairt she's a-fixin' to die."

"Who is she, Elijah?"

He didn't say, but it was plain to me she was the mother of those little children.

"What's her name?"

"I dunno, Missy."

I felt her forehead; it was hot as blue blazes. I tried to wake her up. "Lady? Lady?" But she kept right on breathing shallow and sleeping. I lifted one of her eyelids, and that eyeball looked like glass. Then I felt for her pulse but couldn't find it. Upon my word, her wrist was no bigger around than a broomstick.

"We got to get this girl to emergency quick as we can." I looked up at him. "Who is she?"

"I don't rightly know, Missy. Them's her chillun."

I had gathered that much, but I figured this was not the time to find out all I wanted to know. We had to get moving!

"Elijah, help me get her to the car."

With so little meat on her bones, she was light as a feather. While I climbed down out the boxcar, Elijah held her in his arms, then lowered her down to me. In the daylight she looked like somebody out of one of them concentration camps, her eyes sunk back in her head, her lips drawn back over her teeth. She was a young woman, but the sickness aged her in the face. And all that lifting and carrying her to the car didn't rouse her one bit.

We managed to lay her down in the backseat. "The children can ride up front," I said, and we piled in. Elijah put the oldest boy in the middle and the other two children on his knees. None of them were old enough to go to school. I figured she must've had one baby right after the other.

As we eased down the rutted road, my mind was racing. The nearest hospital was twenty miles away in Carson City. We'd have to drive like crazy to get there. The woman would not have insurance—I didn't even have a name to give them at the desk. Without some kind of ID, medical information and such, the hospital would never admit her. *That is, if we make it to the hospital in time. We could lose this girl before we get to there.*

I looked back to see if she was still breathing. She was. Then I looked at the children. They were dark skinned and had black eyes—just about the prettiest little things I ever seen. The youngest of the three, the girl, was nestled against Elijah's right arm, sucking her thumb, and the boys were teasing each other. Elijah laid his hand on one boy's head, and the teasing stopped.

Once we got down the dirt road and turned onto the highway, I gunned it! Believe you me, I pressed the pedal to the metal, and we were flying with me leaning on the horn passing every car, truck, and vehicle on the road. I was thinking, *Lord, I hope Dr. Elsie is making rounds in the hospital when we get there.*

As we were coming into Carson City, I had to slow down for an intersection. I glanced back and could see the woman was still alive. "Elijah, tell me what you know about this situation."

He waited until the light changed and I was weaving in and out of the traffic before he answered. "Well, Missy, they just straggled along that trestle one day, this young lady and her little'uns. Found that old boxcar and set up in it."

"Where's the daddy?"

"I never seen a man about."

"You don't know her name?"

"No'm. Don't none of them speak English."

"Must be Mexicans. Was she working in town before she got sick?"

Elijah took so long to answer, I thought he didn't hear me.

"I say, did she work in town before she got sick?"

"I reckon she did," he said and clammed up so as to discourage me from asking anything more. But I had to know.

"What do you mean, you reckon she did?" I asked.

"Well, Missy, she worked nights."

"At night? Where?"

Elijah turned his face away from me toward the window.

"You say she worked at night, Elijah?" I pressed.

"Well, Missy, before she got down sick, of an evening, after the chillun were asleep, she'd slip out and be gone till almost daylight."

That's all I needed to know. The woman laying on my backseat was none other than that streetwalker!

"She'd leave those children up there all by theirselves?"

"She knew I was close by. I looked in on them from time to time."

We were getting near the hospital. "I guess she slept all day?"

"No'm. She didn't sleep a lot. Stayed awake as long as she could lookin' after the chillun, but here lately she's been so sick, they been playin' around my place."

When we pulled up at the emergency entrance, I hopped out of the car and went in to get a wheelchair. An orderly and a nurse were dispatched to bring in the patient, while I stood at the desk to fill in the papers.

I had to make up a name. The only Spanish name I could think of was Carmen Miranda, so I wrote that and gave her age as twenty-three. *What difference does it make?* I thought. I didn't have time to answer a lot of questions.

"Does she have Blue Cross?" a big fat nurse asked me.

"I can't tell you that, and the patient's too sick to say, but don't worry about the bill, it'll be paid. Just get Dr. Elsie in here quick as you can. I got to make a call."

An orderly and the other nurse had rolled the wheel-chair inside and were lifting that poor sick girl onto a gurney. I glanced out the door to see if Elijah and the children were okay, and they were. He had them sitting on a bench. Looked like he was entertaining them with a piece of string, making a cat's cradle or something. I knew I would have to move the car directly, but right then I had to get in touch with Pastor Osborne.

The phone rang until the answering machine came on. I hate them things! I left a message, then called Clara.

"Clara, this is Esmeralda. We got a sick woman over here at the Carson City General emergency room. I want you to put her on the prayer chain right away. I got no time for questions, just get her on the list. . . . What's her name? I don't know, but she's the mother of them three children we saw on the tracks. I got to go now. I got to hang up."

The next call I made was to the Spanish teacher, Lucy Mangrum. I figured that if this sick woman became con-scious, we might get some information if we had an inter-preter. Quickly I explained the situation, and Lucy said she'd come right over. But I told her to wait until she heard from me again.

As soon as I hung up the phone, it came to me that Lucy ought to be at the hospital right away. If Carmen woke up, she might not stay awake but a few minutes, and we'd lose the chance to find out what we needed to know. But I couldn't call her back—the security guard was looking in the door to see whose car was parked at the entrance. I started walking over to move it.

Well, I changed my mind again—I didn't much care if I got a ticket. I had to check on Carmen, who was still laying on the gurney. I felt her face—it was dry as a bone. "Nurse!" I yelled. "Get an IV going here. This woman is plum dried out!"

Seeing the big fat one was getting off her chair to see about it, I headed for the door. She called after me. "Who is this Carmen Miranda?"

I stopped, leaned against the door, and looked back at her like she was the dumbest person on the planet. "You don't know who Carmen Miranda is?" I shook my head in disbelief. "Honey, Carmen Miranda is the most famous singer and dancer in the whole U.S. of A.!"

With eyes wide as saucers, that nurse turned to the other nurse, all excited. "Do you know who this patient is? She's Carmen Miranda!"

I was out the door.

By the time I found a parking place and got Cokes out of the vending machine for the children, Pastor Osborne had driven up. He hurried toward me, and we stood outside a few minutes while I filled him in on the situation.

Before he went inside, he spoke to Elijah and gave the children some gum.

Dr. Elsie must've been in the hospital when they paged her, because when we walked in, she was already beside the gurney, her stethoscope on the woman's chest. Seeing us, she put the stethoscope in her pocket and motioned us over as she called to one of the nurses, "See if you can find a room for this patient."

Fat as she was, that nurse fairly skipped to the phone. "Yes, ma'am, I'll get her a room right away," she said with stars in her eyes over having a celebrity for a patient.

Dr. Elsie reached down to read the name on the armband. "Carmen Miranda," she murmured. "Hmm."

"Carmen who?" Pastor Osborne asked.

He got no answer from either of us, and I was sure as shooting hoping he was too young to know who Carmen Miranda was.

Dr. Elsie scribbled orders and handed them across the desk, then turned to Pastor Osborne and me.

The doctor is a woman of few words. She told us that until they ran tests, she could not determine what was wrong with the patient. "This elevation of temperature we may be able to bring down, but the illness is not something that has come on her suddenly. Whatever it is, this woman has been sick for some time. Her lungs are in bad shape, and she's as dry as a bone. We can do something about dehydration, but if it is as serious as I think it is, she's too far gone for help."

My voice trembled a little. "Dr. Elsie, she has three little children . . ."

"Three children?"

"Three, two boys and a girl. The girl is about three years old, I'd say, and the boys are maybe four and five."

Dr. Elsie looked grim. "Where are they?"

"Outside with Elijah."

The nurse put down the phone and turned to us. "As soon as we can move a patient, Dr. Elsie, we'll have a private room for Miss Miranda." She was so pleased with herself, she looked like she might sprout wings. "Three nineteen, third floor," she said. "That's a corner room with windows on two sides—the best room in the hospital, I believe."

She had hardly finished telling us this when the room became available. The two nurses must've argued over which one would go with Carmen, because I heard the one with the weight problem say, "Well, I made the call!" She must've been the winner. The orderly started rolling the gurney toward the elevator, and she chased after him.

As the gurney rattled down the hall, Dr. Elsie asked Pastor Osborne to come to her office so we could pray.

As always, that man knew exactly how to pray—not like he was delivering a professional duty but like he was an awestruck man full of worship. He addressed the Great Physician and thanked him for whatever he was going to do for Carmen. Then he prayed for Dr. Elsie to be given good judgment and for me and Elijah to know how to help and have the strength to do it. Then he prayed so tenderly for those three little children, I had to squeeze back tears.

When he was done praying, I could see his eyes were watery too. Dr. Elsie reached up and patted him on the shoulder. "There's nothing more you and Esmeralda can do here right now. You need to go take care of those lit-tle ones. I'll walk you to the door."

Seeing the children all curled up on the bench with Elijah, Dr. Elsie shook her head. "It doesn't look good, Esmeralda. We'll know something in a day or two. We'll do everything we can for . . . for Carmen Miranda."

That's the only time I ever saw Dr. Elsie wink.

14

After seeing to Carmen, the next thing we had to do was find a place for the children. That wasn't hard—Pastor Osborne said he would take them home with him. I knew this would tickle Betty Osborne to death.

I helped Elijah put the kids in the backseat of the pastor's car. Then Elijah crawled in the front seat while I held the door open. "Pastor Osborne will take you home, Elijah."

"No'm. I'm going with the chillun. It'll be a strange place for them, and they need me to spend a little time with them till they settle in. Then I'll get along home."

Pastor Osborne spoke up. "Good. That'll help Betty. But Elijah, you needn't to walk home; whenever you're ready to go, I'll drive you."

"What should I do if I need you, Elijah?" I asked.

"Maybe you could call me at the preacher's house."

"Sure," the pastor said. "Esmeralda, you have our number."

"Yes, I have it. . . . Okay, then, Elijah, if you aren't at the Osbornes', I'll find you at home. Might be I have to send somebody else, though. I think I need to stay right here at the hospital."

I closed the car door, and they eased on around the driveway. Watching them go, I wished I could be there to see Betty's face when those kids arrived. She would light up like a Christmas tree.

I looked across the parking lot and saw Lucy Mangrum getting out of her car. I waited for her.

"Esmeralda, I couldn't stay put," she said as she hurried up to me. "What if that lady wakes up and I'm not there?"

"It's good you came. Let's go up and see her."

When we reached Carmen's room, they were still bathing and dressing her. As we stood in the hall, I filled Lucy in on all that was going on. I had to let her in on the fact that Carmen Miranda was not the woman's real name. Lucy said that if Carmen spoke Spanish, she would try to find out what her name really was.

Finally we were admitted in the room. There were tubes going in and out that poor emaciated body, and the girl was still unconscious. We'd hardly sat down when there they came to take her down to X ray.

While Carmen was gone, I went down the hall and called Clara to bring her up-to-date on the situation. "Tell the women not to be calling the hospital. I'll call you if there's any change." Once the W.W.s heard the children were at Betty's, I knew they'd go over there with food and help the Osbornes any way they could.

The chair I sat in was not the most comfortable, but after they brought Carmen back to the room, I had reason to stand by her bedside. She was mumbling and from time to time opening her eyes, though I'm not sure she was seeing anything. She was kind of wild and talking out of her head. Still, I told Lucy to listen and ask what her name was.

Lucy tried. It was no use. The woman was not in her right mind.

The one thing that made me smile that day was them nurses. They could not have been nicer. They brought me a better chair—a big, soft recliner. Sometimes there were as many as two of them and an aide in the room, fussing over Carmen, sponging her off, checking the IVs, taking her pulse.

Of course, they were being so nice because of Carmen's celebrity status. Once they used up every excuse they could think of for staying in the room, they stood around, asking me questions about Carmen. "Was she on Broadway?" "What movies did she play in?" "How many times was she married?" "Who was she married to?" I tell you, that put me on the spot. I reckon a born liar could've handled it, but I for one am not a born liar. I just told them this was not the time nor the place to be asking such questions.

But by then, the news that a celebrity was on the third floor had spread to the next shift coming on duty. As soon as the shift changed, Lucy and I had a fresh crop of nurses making a beeline to Room 319, hoping to get a glimpse of Carmen Miranda. I tell you, it just plain wore me out.

A Christian don't get away with lying. I felt so guilty, but I couldn't tell them nurses the truth because Carmen had no kind of insurance, and hospitals are fussy about money. Still, as Splurgeon says, "A clear conscience is a good pillow." And my conscience was far from clear.

So I just concentrated on the business at hand. Since Lucy didn't want to leave the room to get something to eat, I went down to the cafeteria, ate one of them sorry hospital meals, and brought her a plate. Carmen was still very restless, but we hoped this was a sign she was getting a little better.

However, after supper, when Dr. Elsie looked in on her, she just shook her head. "The next twenty-four hours are crucial. I would've put her in intensive care, but we're filled up in there. Keep a close eye, Esmeralda, and if you need me, I can be here in two shakes of a lamb's tail."

That was a comfort. The white coat and the stethoscope made Dr. Elsie seem like a different person from the woman in a shirtmaker dress who sat on the third pew in Apostolic Bible Church.

"I'm afraid it'll be a long night for you," she said. "Can I get you anything?" After we said no, she reached over and hugged us both. I tell you, the white coat could not hide the heart of the saint in a shirtmaker dress.

A little after eleven o'clock, five nurses came into the room, whispering amongst theirselves. Above their whispering, I heard a tap on the door. Pastor Osborne poked his head in the room. "Is this a bad time?" he said.

"No, come in," I said.

He slipped into the room. "What are all these nurses doing in here?"

"Well, I don't know, really," I lied. Of course, I knew they had come to see the star of stage, screen, and television. It was downright crazy. Carmen was sleeping more peacefully now, but those women were bumping into each other, trying to find something to do so as to stay in the room. Before they started asking ridiculous questions, I took the pastor into the hall where we could talk.

I asked about the children. He said Betty had bathed and fed them, then he had told them stories and helped Betty put them to bed in the spare room. Sometime in the late afternoon, he had taken Elijah home with more than enough food for his supper. "The W.W.s brought over casseroles to last a week," the pastor said. "While they were there, we all got down on our knees in the living room and prayed for Carmen."

I felt guilty for not telling him Carmen was not her real name. I started to tell him, but I chickened out. "Pastor, I just wanted to tell you how much it means to me having you praying for her and us. Also, the good messages you bring us every Sunday. Like Splurgeon says, 'Good pastures make fat sheep.'"

The minute I said it, I knew I was not a fat sheep; for all I was worth, I was a black sheep for sure.

After Pastor Osborne left, Lucy and I settled in for the night. I slept very little, because the hospital staff kept coming in all during the night. Then, at a little before five o'clock, we started hearing ambulances. One after another of them was coming, their sirens screaming.

Well, I couldn't worry about what was going on. Lucy and I had enough on our hands without anything more.

But after five o'clock, when we really needed a nurse, they were all tied up with that emergency, whatever it was. Carmen was thrashing about in the bed, pulling at the side rails and trying to get out. It took both of us to hold her down. She was babbling something, and Lucy said she was asking for her babies. That was a good sign, but Carmen was getting wilder by the minute.

We sure needed some help, but now I figure it was a good thing we couldn't get a nurse, because that was when we got Carmen's real name.

It's amazing the strength of a person at death's door. As I was trying to keep the poor girl from doing harm to herself, she dug her fingernails into my arm and would not let go. Frantic, she stared at me and asked something. I looked over to Lucy.

"She wants to know who you are," Lucy told me.

"Tell her I'm her friend." I hesitated. "And ask her to let go my arm."

Lucy relayed all that information, but Carmen did not let go.

"Tell her the children are safe—that they are with the preacher until she can get well."

"I did already, but it doesn't quiet her."

"Well, ask her what her name is, then."

Carmen mumbled something that Lucy bent to hear. Then Lucy looked up with a smile. "She says it's Maria Lopez."

I was able to free my arm. As I stood there examining the marks her nails had made, I said, "Ask her where she comes from."

Lucy asked, but now Maria was jerking like she was having a seizure. I went out in the hall and hollered, "Get me a nurse in here right away!"

I didn't see a nurse anywhere, not even at the nurses' station. A maintenance worker at the far end of the hall put down her mop and came toward me. She was as big around as she was tall. "Call Dr. Elsie," I told her. "Tell her it's Carmen." The woman shuffled off down the hall, but I didn't trust her to do what I asked.

I looked in the room to see if it was safe for me to go find somebody. Maria was still jerking and had wet the bed, but she was not so violent as she had been before. "Lucy," I said, "there's not a nurse on this floor. I'm trying to get hold of a nurse."

"Wait a minute," Lucy said, sounding about to panic. "Don't leave me right now."

Maria was coming out of the seizure, if that's what it was. She lay there exhausted, making a gurgling sound in her throat.

"Well, then we got to change this bed," I said. I went to find sheets. The maintenance woman unlocked a closet, handed me a gown, and piled my arms with sheets, pillowcases, towels, and washcloths.

Back in the room, I cleaned up Maria, then put a folded sheet under her and showed Lucy how to lift her and remove the wet sheet. It took a while, but we managed to have Maria in a nice clean bed by the time a nurse finally showed up.

With a nurse in the room, I figured it was all right for me to make the call to Dr. Elsie. I went out in the hall to use the phone. When I got ahold of Dr. Elsie, I gave her a blow-by-blow description of the night's activity. She laughed at the nurses' curiosity about Carmen Miranda. "Esmeralda, she's been dead since the fifties!"

"I know," I said, "but that's the only Spanish name I could think of, and you know the hospital would never admit a patient that had no name. They might keep her in emergency a day and a night, but after that, they'd like as not ship her out."

Dr. Elsie chuckled. "In the meantime, she's getting the royal treatment!"

"Well, yes," I said. "I'm not too proud about that, but it was the best I could do."

When I got back in the room, Maria was sleeping and Lucy looked like a very happy camper. "Maria is from Guatemala," she told me, wringing her hands. "All her family were killed in an earthquake down there. I don't know what brought her here. She's real agitated about her kids. I kept telling her they're safe and sound." She stopped wringing her hands and looked down at them. She was quiet for a moment. "Esmeralda, do you think the Lord is going to heal her?"

"I hope so," I said, but I had my doubts.

I was fixing to go downstairs for a bite of breakfast when Dr. Elsie came. She read the chart, which didn't have much written on it, then checked Maria from head to toe.

"Dr. Elsie, what do you think?" I asked.

"I think the fluids have helped, but she still needs to be in ICU. There's been a train wreck in Sumter County with injuries filling every bed, so we'll have to keep her here." She turned to Lucy. "Have you found out anything more than her name?"

"She's from Guatemala. All her family were killed in an earthquake."

"I see." She jotted something on the chart, tucked it under her arm, and told us, "I'm ordering another sedative. If she gets out of hand, call the nurse."

Lucy and I spent another long day at the hospital. Nurses were so busy with the emergency patients, they didn't have time to pay attention to Maria. I kept close watch on the IVs, and when one needed to be changed, I made it my business to find a nurse. Maria slept all day, so in the afternoon, I sent Lucy home to take a shower, make some phone calls, and rest for a bit. In two hours she was back at the hospital and gave me my turn.

I took a bath, put on fresh clothes, and fed the birds. I was ready to drive back to the hospital when the phone rang. It was Beatrice. I didn't have time to tell her the whole story, so I just told her I was sitting in the hospital with a friend she didn't know. She didn't press me, because she was too excited about what she had to say.

"Esmeralda, Carl said he would go to church with me Sunday. What do you think?"

"Well, I think that's fine."

"I know, but you know how people are—they'll be looking at us and whispering and asking me to introduce him."

"Well, go to church a little late, sit in the back, and leave fast."

"But if we go late, all the back-row seats will be filled up."

I sighed. That woman could not think for herself, and I was too tired to do her thinking for her. "Beatrice, you're just going to have to do what you think is best. I have got to get back to the hospital."

"Wait! Just one thing more, Esmeralda. When he brings me home, do I invite him in or just let him go on his way?"

"Why don't you invite him for dinner?"

"For dinner! It won't look right, me bringing a man in the house with nobody here but me."

I tell you, I was put out with her. "Well, then ask somebody else to eat dinner with you."

"I never thought of that. There's lots of people hungry after church."

"Well, you do that, Beatrice. I got to go now. I'll talk to you later."

As I drove back to the hospital, I figured I'd been short with Beatrice. But for the life of me, I just didn't have it in me to feel bad about that. There she was, hanging on the phone like she was the only person in the world who had a care, and there I was, facing so many problems I couldn't keep my head above water. If I hadn't cared about her, I would've told her, "Beatrice, you are on your own!" But I knew I was thinking that way only because I was tired. When the whole mess was over, I'd be there for Beatrice, like I'd always been.

When I stepped on the elevator, there was Dr. Elsie. She did not mince her words. "Esmeralda, we need to talk."

When we got off at the third floor, she took me to a deserted waiting room, and we sat down.

"I hate to tell you this," she said, "but the hospital is going to dismiss Maria Lopez. With all these emergency patients, the administration is going to put two beds and two cots in Maria's room. Even if I could persuade them to keep her, Maria is too sick to be in a room with three other patients. Besides, the administrator told me her records are incomplete and that it's against all the rules of the company to admit a patient, much less keep one, whose paperwork is incomplete. In fact, he says he'd like to dismiss the nurses who allowed this to happen, but he can't do without them right now because of all these emergencies."

"Well, thank you for telling me," I said.

Dr. Elsie peered at me, maybe wondering why I was taking this news so well. "What will you do, Esmeralda?"

"I'll take her home to my house."

15

Dr. Elsie had us get a hospital bed and other equipment for Maria. She also got in touch with a hospice center, and a worker there agreed to visit and help out. But mainly the nursing was left up to me and Lucy, who was the only person who could communicate with Maria.

When I had a chance to leave the sickroom for a few minutes, I organized how we would handle the situation. I put Clara in charge of running errands, shopping for groceries, all that kind of thing. I knew she would ask the W.W.s to furnish meals for us and whoever else happened to be in the house. Thelma could be a backup for Lucy or me when one of us had to catch a few hours of sleep. I also would ask her to find someone to take care of Mrs. Purdy on Fridays, since I wouldn't be able to do that for a while. With all the diarrhea Maria was having, I knew the laundry would get out of hand. If I couldn't handle it, Mabel Elmwood had a maid who could help out.

I didn't want to lose my garden, but I knew I could count on Elijah to take care of it if somebody would give him transportation. I wrote myself a note to ask Boris to go for him and take him home. Matter of fact, my beans were coming in, and Boris's young people could help Elijah pick them. They could also keep the grass cut. I didn't have to worry about canning the beans or whatever produce came in; the W.W.s were so anxious to help, they'd can the stuff the day it was picked.

I put in a quick call to Thelma, told her what I needed people to do, and asked her to pass the word. I also asked her to call Beatrice and tell her the whole story of what was going on with us now. By the time I put the phone down, help certainly was on the way—the next day things were buzzing around my place.

The hospice people were in and out, offering every kind of service you could imagine. They were wonderful people, I tell you. Lucy and I couldn't sing their praises enough. I wish they'd been around when Bud was sick.

But the backbone of our operation was Dr. Elsie. She came every day and whenever I needed her, day or night. Another one we couldn't have done without was Pastor Osborne. That dear man would slip in, sometimes late at night, and we'd find him kneeling beside the bed, holding Maria's hand and praying. He came every day, sometimes more than once a day. I was certain he'd come if I needed him in an emergency.

And an emergency was what we had on our hands one afternoon, not long after I had brought Maria home with me.

Well, it wasn't a life-or-death emergency, but Maria was wild-eyed, in a frenzy about her children. I watched her a few minutes as she grabbed at Lucy and jabbered in that unknown tongue.

Lucy told me what she was saying. "She keeps asking over and over for Angelica."

"Angelica? That must be her little girl." I didn't think Maria was in any condition to have the children visit her. But then again, maybe it would calm her down if she saw them.

Sometimes you just don't know what's best.

I went to the phone and called the Osbornes. "Betty, this is Esmeralda. Can you get those children over here right away?"

"Right away? You're not going to put them in foster care, are you?"

"No, their mama needs to see them."

"Oh. Well, the boys are outside playing catch with my husband, but I'll get them in here. Bob will take them and the little girl to you as quick as he can."

After I hung up with Betty, I went back in the room to report what she'd said. Lucy was trying to get the bedpan under Maria, but we soon found out she was too late. What a mess we had to clean up! I was on my way to the laundry room with the dirty sheets when Pastor Osborne drove up.

I tell you, those children never looked so good. They were scrubbed clean, their hair was cut and combed, and the clothes they were wearing would've made any discount store proud. Those were three beautiful children.

I looked in on Maria, and she seemed limp as a dishrag. "Bring 'em on in here," I told the pastor.

Seeing their mother, the boys dashed across the room and jumped up on the bed. "Oh, now, see here," I said, but I hushed when I saw it was okay. Maria looked dazed, and the boys calmed down a bit. Feebly, she lifted her arms to hug them. The boys kept kissing her face and talking a mile a minute.

Lucy whispered, "They're asking her when she will get well."

Maria was too weak to do more than murmur through her pale lips. The boys started laughing and pointing at the pastor. Lucy explained. "Now they're telling her about eating ice cream and playing catch and the pastor splitting his pants!"

Pastor Osborne smiled. "Lucy, tell them it's their sister's turn." When Lucy told them, both boys flung their arms around their mother's neck, hugging and kissing her, not wanting to let go.

I took hold of one boy's arm. "Leggo," I said, tugging at him. Reluctantly, he let go, and then his brother did too. The boys scrambled to the foot of the bed, sat crosslegged with their chins resting on their fists, and waited to see what Angelica would do.

Pastor Osborne lifted the little girl over the side rails, careful not to get her tangled up in all the intravenous stuff, and gently placed her in her mother's arms. Well, you just never know what a child is gonna do. Angelica burst into tears! And poor Maria was helpless to comfort her. The frightened child just got louder! The boys moved quickly to pacify their sister, but it was no use. She just kept right on screaming.

The pastor had to lift Angelica back over the rails and stand her down beside the bed. Only then did she stop screaming. Now she was sobbing and clinging to the pastor's leg. Pastor Osborne stroked her head and did the best he could to comfort her, but as he looked across the bed to me, he mouthed the words *I guess we better go.*

Still, he just stood there, not having the heart to take those little things from their mother.

After a while, Angelica quieted a bit. Pastor Osborne took out his handkerchief and helped her blow her nose. Then, with her thumb in her mouth and still leaning against the pastor's knee, she stood staring at her mother.

Maria's sick eyes were fixed on that beautiful little tear-stained face. Reaching with her finger, she touched the ringlets of Angelica's hair, touched her cheek, her lips, and murmured softly. The child sniffled, a sob catching in her throat.

Before a fresh flood of tears could start, I gave Lucy a sign, and she told the boys to say good-bye to their mother. They began planting big wet kisses all over Maria's face. Finally, I beckoned to them, and they crawled off the bed.

Pastor Osborne gently herded the three of them to the door. I watched Maria as her eyes followed them. When the door closed, she turned her face to the wall.

I asked Lucy if she had gotten the names of the boys from Maria. She had; they were Rios and Carlos.

I hurried outside to catch the pastor before he got away. He was standing on the porch, Angelica in his arms, her head nestled against his neck and shoulder. The boys had run ahead and jumped in the car.

"Pastor," I said, waving my finger, "one of them boys is named Carlos and the other one Rios. You'll have to figure out which one is which."

He smiled. "That won't be hard." He called after the boys. "Carlos?" The older one poked his head out the window. *"Muy bien,"* Pastor Osborne said. He turned to me with a sheepish smile. "Those are the only two Spanish words I know."

As I watched the pastor and the children pull out of the driveway, I couldn't help but grieve for Maria. I tell you, to think of that dying mother leaving those precious babies was more than I could take. I went back in the kitchen and tried to get hold of myself. I guess it was because I was so tired, but I started crying and couldn't stop. I cried and cried.

In an effort to get control of myself, I made a cup of tea and tried to think of other things.

I stood at the sink and looked out the window at Elijah talking to the young people and showing them how to pick the beans. I thought about the tiller. Unbeknownst to me, Clara had asked the class if she could use the carpet money to pay for the tiller, and they had all agreed. Now I needed to ask somebody to bring it up to my house and put it in the shed until I could find Elijah some way of hauling it around town. But there was too much going on, and I was too wore out to figure that out.

Boris was cutting the grass. I stepped outside and hollered to him. He shut off the mower and came to the porch, wiping his hands on his blue jeans. My eyes must've been all red and puffy, because he put his arm around my shoulders. "Oh, Miss Esmeralda, I'm so sorry. Can't I do something for you?"

Well, he didn't do nothing for me but bring on another flood of tears. I had a tissue in my pocket, so I blew my nose and got hold of myself before I said, "Let's go inside."

He held the screen door for me and followed me into the kitchen.

"Boris, the ladies have brought so much food in here, I don't have room in the refrigerator to keep it. See here." I pointed to the food crowding my countertops. "Now, it's almost lunchtime; you get a couple of the girls in here to make the tea and fix barbecue sandwiches. But do tell them to keep it down. Where there's sickness, we have to have quiet. There's plenty of ice, and somebody brought paper cups, paper plates, and napkins. Elijah can come in here, but the rest of you can have a picnic out there under that live oak."

"Yes, ma'am. I understand."

I gave his arm a squeeze and sent him back outside. Before going into Maria's room, I splashed a lot of cold water on my face.

Lucy was sitting beside Maria's bed, looking tuckered out. The odor wasn't good in the room, so I raised a window and sprayed around with disinfectant. A breeze stirred the curtains and kept them kind of dancing. They were some white ones I'd bought on sale several years before, and I still think they were the prettiest I ever had.

"Lucy, Maria is sleeping. Why don't you go in my bedroom and lie down?"

Lucy stretched and yawned. "I think I will."

The sound of the lawn mower started up again.

Left alone with Maria, I watched her sleep, her mouth open, her breathing irregular. It reminded me of Bud's last days; the only difference was that his breathing had been loud and raspy.

It had taken me a long time before I could think of Bud any way but sick. Now I could think of him healthy like he once was, but tending a sick person brought back all those bad memories.

I heaved a big sigh, but the heaviness hung in my chest worse than the pain of heartburn.

I wondered how much longer Maria could hold out. I folded the newspaper and fanned her face. "Lord," I whispered, "for the sake of those precious little ones, won't you spare this mother's life?"

I could hear the girls tiptoeing in the kitchen, closing cabinet doors, talking quietly. I'd let them finish before I fixed a plate for Elijah.

Some young voices singing in the garden floated through the window, sounding sweet, like so many little birds waking you up of a morning. Hearing sounds of life being lived outside and at the same time waiting for a spirit to leave a body made the heaviness I was feeling even heavier. How much we take for granted . . . how soon the living is over.

I heard a car drive up, and I looked out the window. It was Pastor Osborne. I didn't get up—he always let himself in.

A moment later, he eased into the room and pulled up a chair beside mine. We nodded to each other, and I began fanning Maria again. She looked too worn out ever to wake up.

"Pastor, is she all right—is little Angelica all right?"

"Yeah. On the way home, with that little thumb in her mouth, she nearly fell asleep. As I left the house just now, Betty had her and the boys out at the picnic table, getting ready to eat watermelon."

We sat at Maria's bedside, not saying anything for a long time. I was wondering why he'd come back so soon. I figured he must've known how I was feeling and just came back to be with me.

"You know, Pastor Osborne," I finally said, "it just don't seem fair for this young mama to die and leave those three babies. Why don't he take me? I've almost lived my three score and ten."

He didn't say anything.

"We've all prayed for Maria to live, but to tell the truth, I don't think she will."

He still didn't say anything. Some preachers would've ripped out a sermonette about how we must have faith, and that if we didn't have hope, then we didn't have faith because faith and hope go together. All of which I have understood since I was knee-high to a grasshopper.

But Pastor Osborne isn't like that. He's not what you would call a professional preacher with a fancy D.Min. behind his name, out hobnobbing with the country-club set. As much as I look up to the man, I feel as close to him as I would to the son I never had. I can dump on him my worst feelings and know he'll only talk to God about me.

"Pastor, you know about my husband, Bud, getting wounded in the war and all?"

He nodded.

"Well, when he went off to war, I prayed my heart out that no harm would come to him. It was a bitter pill to swallow when he come back a basket case. But I didn't give up. Every day and night I prayed with faith and hope that God would give us a miracle. But we never did get one."

Pastor Osborne knew I was asking for help; still, he didn't hurry to oblige. He took the newspaper out of my hand and swatted at a fly. "Did I get him?"

I didn't know, or care. I wanted him to go ahead and tell me what he thought.

He handed the paper back to me. "Esmeralda, these things are hard to understand. . . . My daddy always told me that we must let God know some things we don't know. . . . He said if we knew everything the Lord knows, then he wouldn't be God."

"I've thought of that," I said. "But . . ."

He shifted in his chair to see me better. The way the sun was coming in the window, the light was circling his head and I could hardly see his face.

"You know what's helped me, Esmeralda? Jesus. He never performed a miracle just for himself . . . never used his power for his own advantage . . ."

I'd thought of that many times too. I'd thought about him fasting forty days and then the old devil coming to him, tempting him to turn stones into bread. As a child, I'd wished he'd shown the devil a thing or two, just up and made hot rolls for himself—with butter and jam!

I wasn't sure what Pastor Osborne was getting at, but I was beginning to see a glimmer.

"Esmeralda, I know you know this—you know that Jesus could've called down legions of angels that night in the garden when they were arresting him, but he didn't. He just never used supernatural means to escape suffering. I hope I'm making sense."

"No," I said, "but go on."

"Well, what I'm trying to say is there were purposes to be served by the things Jesus suffered, and that's why he didn't interfere by using supernatural power."

I still didn't see where he was going. Maybe I was just too tired to think.

"There are purposes served by the things we suffer too."

"Name one!"

He smiled. "Well, the Bible says Jesus learned obedience through the things that he suffered."

I was ashamed of myself. "I'm sorry I spoke out like that, Pastor. It just popped out. . . . What you're saying is . . ."

"What I'm saying is that maybe the best thing we learn from suffering is obedience."

Well, I thought we'd gotten way off the track from why the Lord was not sparing Maria.

Pastor Osborne stretched his long legs in front of him and put his thumbs under his suspenders. "I don't mind telling you, Esmeralda, unanswered prayer is the hardest experience of my life, and there are times when it's awful hard. The thing that helps me is to remember that Jesus once prayed that that cup would pass from him—but it didn't."

Maria groaned. I got up to see about her. She was all right.

Pastor Osborne sat there a long time before he said anything more. But we were both still thinking. We must've been thinking along the same line, because he spoke, as much to himself as to me.

"Faith for a miracle is easier to come by than trusting the Lord when no miracle happens. . . . I'm not telling you anything you don't already know, am I?"

"No, you aren't, Pastor," I said. "With Bud, things didn't turn up roses, and though it took some time, I got to the place where I was willing to trust the Lord that he loved us and that he had some reason for Bud's not getting well."

Lucy came back in the room just then, rubbing her eyes. "Hello, Preacher Bob. Esmeralda, that nap felt real good. Maria looks quiet. Why don't you go in and have a little siesta now?"

I glanced out the window. "The young people are eating out under the tree. If you'll excuse me, Pastor, I'll go in the kitchen and fix Elijah's lunch."

"Oh, I've got to be going," he said as he stood up. "Is there anything I can do for you ladies?"

"You've already done a lot for me, Pastor," I told him. I felt like giving him a hug, but I didn't.

Elijah was on the back porch. I told him to go in the bathroom and wash up. When he came back to the table, I handed him a plate and asked him to choose whatever he wanted from the casseroles I had put out. He looked them over, kind of sniffed, then asked, "Missy, where's the grits?"

I laughed and put on a pot. "How 'bout I fix you some sausage and eggs to go with those grits?"

"Oh, Missy! Would you do that for me?"

I stopped what I was doing, put both hands flat on the table before him, and looked him square in the eye. "Elijah, there ain't nothing in the world I wouldn't do for you."

"I know, Missy. I know."

Dr. Elsie had promised to let me know the results of the tests. I thought she would call me when they came back, but the next morning her car rolled up in my driveway. I met her out on the porch.

She took a seat on the glider, then patted the seat next to her. "Esmeralda, what we have here is a full-blown case of AIDS—the last stages. There's nothing we can do but make Maria as comfortable as we can."

"AIDS?" Well, I couldn't say I was too surprised. "What's the danger of our catching it from Maria?"

Dr. Elsie shook her head. "Quite unlikely," she said. "The virus is transmitted through bodily fluids, but casual personal contact is not dangerous. If you had a cut and got her blood on it, you could contract the disease that way. Sharing infected needles is another way."

"What about the children?"

"We'll have them tested. That, of course, is real cause for concern. With vaginal deliveries there's danger, and breast milk can transmit the virus too. Let's just pray that they test negative. If they don't, well, we'll cross that bridge when we come to it."

She stood up and went inside to check on Maria. I waited on the porch and worried about those precious children. Even if by some miracle they weren't born with the virus, there was every reason to believe they could get it by being in such close contact with their mama. All I could think of was those little boys kissing Maria. If only I had known . . .

My mind was running around in my head like a merry-go-round. I'd had it all planned that the Osbornes would adopt the children. But if the poor little things were going to have the virus, it would be too much for the Osbornes to take on. *Oh, Lord, have mercy!*

Dr. Elsie was coming out the door. "Esmeralda, Maria won't last much longer. That means we must not waste any time taking care of the business this situation poses. Right now, we don't need to worry about expenses, the hospital and funeral; that's the least of our worries. Lucy says Maria isn't a citizen of this country, so there's red tape involved in anything we may do relative to her or the children. I'd like to keep them out of foster care as long as we can, but if Maria should die suddenly, some bureaucrat might even send them back to Guatemala."

I could feel my throat tighten. I did not like the sound of that one bit.

Dr. Elsie put her hand on my arm. "I want Lucy to find out everything she can about Maria. I know she said all her family was killed in an earthquake, but Maria didn't have these babies by herself, you know. Somewhere there's a father. We have to track him down."

"We'll get on it right away," I told her, but for the life of me, I didn't know the first thing about tracking down a man whose name we might not ever know. Especially if Maria had always been a loose woman with many partners.

16

❧

Maria had a bad night, but after it was over, she rallied remarkably. I'd told Lucy everything Dr. Elsie had told me, and she said she would try to get as much information out of Maria as she could. Hospice was coming that day, and I had called Thelma to come, too, so I felt they could spare me for a few hours while I drove up to the county courthouse.

After being shut up in the house for so many days, it felt good to be driving up the highway by myself. With my cruise control set at fifty-five, which was the speed limit along that stretch of the road, I was breezing along, thinking about the business up ahead. Just outside the city limits, I heard a siren and glanced at my rearview mirror. Lo and behold, a cruiser was on my bumper, the blue light flashing!

I pulled over on the shoulder, wondering what was wrong with my car. None of the lights on the dash were lit up. It didn't feel like I had a flat or anything. I rolled down the window and waited for the officer. Then I looked up and saw who it was. Horace Thigpen!

Without looking at me, he asked for my driver's license. I felt my face growing red as I searched for it. My pocketbook was always a bottomless pit. I finally dug out my wallet, and the license was in it.

I handed it to him, and he read it like I was some total stranger. I tell you, I was furious. Did he think he could arrest me and convince a judge I was a drug dealer posing as a God-fearing woman?

He jotted something down and asked for my vehicle registration.

"What's this about, Horace?"

"Speeding."

"Speeding? I had my cruise control at fifty-five."

He handed back the registration. "Then your cruise control is out of calibration, Miss Esmeralda."

The nerve of him!

"Horace Thigpen, there is nothing wrong with my cruise control, and you know it! You just spotted my car and come after me for no reason but to harass the life outta me."

He grinned. "You wouldn't resist an officer of the law, now would you, Miss Esmeralda?"

"Officer of the law? You're nothing but your daddy's deputy, and if I have to take you to court over this, I will."

"My word against yours, Miss Esmeralda."

I could've slapped that grin right off his face.

"Well, fine then. Write the ticket and be quick about it. I'm in a hurry to get to the county courthouse."

He scribbled the ticket and tore it off the pad. "So you do admit you're in a great big hurry?"

As I looked up at him, ready to give him another piece of my mind, it dawned on me that somebody ought to tell him about Maria. There wasn't anybody but Lucy, Dr. Elsie, and me who knew enough to tell. And I was the only one knew he'd slept with her.

"Horace," I began, "that woman you . . . well, her name is Maria. I hate telling you this, but she's dying of AIDS."

That wiped the grin off his face. "AIDS?" he repeated, his face gone pale. "I don't believe you. You're just saying that so I'll tear up this ticket."

"Hand me the ticket, Horace."

He gave it to me, his hand trembling.

"Now do you believe me?" I asked.

His face grew white as cotton. "How did you find out she has AIDS?"

"She's laying sick in my house right now. You can go up there and see for yourself."

"At your house? How? Why . . . ?" He was so white I was afraid he was going to faint.

"It's a long story, and I don't have time to answer a bunch of questions. Now, if you'll please step aside, I'll be on my way."

"Gimme back that ticket. I won't charge you."

"Not on your life, Buster. Not until you apologize for the rotten trick you tried to pull on me."

"I apologize! I apologize!" He swore and snatched the ticket out of my hand.

I stepped on the accelerator and left him standing in the road. Well, all I had to say was he better go take that test.

As I got going again, I felt bad I had been sharp with him. *I hope and pray he don't have AIDS.* I knew Horace when he was a little boy—use to run around my place chasing my chickens—and his mama was a sweet woman. Horace was the apple of her eye. If she had lived, he would have turned out better than he had. *I sure hope he's okay. Lord, I know he's done wrong, but have mercy on him.* I was thinking maybe this scare would bring him to the Lord.

After I prayed for him, I put Horace behind me and forgot about the speed limit as I zoomed up the road. Being stopped that way didn't leave me much time to do all I had to do. First and foremost, I had to see about finding the daddy. Second on the list was tracking down birth certificates for the children, if they even had birth certificates. And what about burying Maria? Could we bury a foreigner without breaking the law? But probably the most important thing I needed to know was how to get those children adopted by good parents.

I didn't feel equipped to do all this, but who else was there? *Time is of the essence,* I thought. *I'll take the bull by the horns, and if it's the last thing I do, I'll see to it those precious children are spared the clutches of big government.*

"Lord," I said aloud, "help me keep ahead of all them bureaucrats sniffing out cases like this one."

At the courthouse they kept sending me from one office to another. I had to be cagey, not tell them everything, lest they turn me over to Social Services and take everything out of my hands.

The first question I asked got an answer that scared the daylights out of me. I inquired of some bored-looking clerk what the government did with immigrants who didn't have their citizenship papers yet. He looked at me as if I were from outer space. "Illegal aliens are deported."

Smart alec! He looked like something from outer space himself. I could tell he loved his work; he seemed about ready to lie down beside it and go to sleep. Splurgeon said it right: "Idle people are dead people that you can't bury."

I went down the hall, looking for another likely source of help. I saw a sign that said PROBLEM RESOLUTION OFFICE. Sounded like a winner. There were a lot of people waiting, and I had to take a number. I don't know how long I sat there, maybe forty-five minutes, before my number came up. Turns out the people in that office only solve IRS problems. Some skinny woman sent me to Health and Human Services. They gave me forms to fill out that made no sense at all. I asked a woman filing her fingernails if I was in the right place. She said, "It's the right place if you're a Medicaid client." Seeing I was about to blow a gasket, she said, "You probably need the Social Security Administration down the hall."

By the time I got there and sat in the waiting room another half an hour, I was frazzled. Seeing how worn out I was, a woman about my age came around the counter, took me in a private office, and had me sit down across the desk from her. *Anybody that kind must be trustworthy,* I thought, and before I knew it, I was telling her the whole truth, nothing but the truth, so help me God.

She listened carefully, and when I was finished, she said, "What you need is a private investigator. He'll find the father and the birth certificates. You also need a lawyer. I don't know much about adopting foreign-born children, but there's a couple in my church adopted a child from China. I'll find out what I can from them. Give me your phone number, and if I come across anything helpful, I'll get back with you." She stood up and reached her hand across the desk to shake mine. "Miss Esmeralda, I'll be praying for you and that family."

Can you believe a saint like that works for the Social Security Administration! All the way home, I thanked the Lord for her. Now I knew what to do—get us a private eye and a lawyer. Of course, that was going to cost big bucks, but the Lord always provided. I didn't ever worry about money.

I sailed home in record time.

Lucy met me at the door, just beaming. "Esmeralda, guess what? I got some information today. When Thelma was trying to get a little Jell-O in Maria, I was able to ask a few questions. Little by little, she gave me a few answers. I kinda had to piece together what she told me."

"Go on."

"Well, it seems that after the earthquake in Guatemala, Maria and her boyfriend joined a band of migrant workers coming to the States. They were a rough bunch, stealing and drinking, fighting. After they slipped across the border, they had to avoid the law. That's why Maria never went to a hospital to deliver her babies. The best I understand, she was alone in a field when Angelica was born."

"How long have they been in the States?"

"I'm not quite sure, but all of her children were born here. One year they worked in California, but the migrants murdered a woman and had to run from the law. They worked their way through Texas. That's when Maria's boyfriend started doing drugs. He beat her too, but because she didn't speak English and didn't have a green card, there was no way she could get away from him."

"How awful for poor Maria!"

Lucy nodded. "I know. And when they moved from Florida up the east coast, following the crops, they stole a van, and her boyfriend held up a store. By the time they reached the South Carolina border, Maria knew they'd be caught, and she was terrified she might lose her children. Then one morning she found her boyfriend dead in a ditch from an overdose."

"Mercy me, Lucy, you got a lot of information! Do you know how she got to Live Oaks?"

"Yeah, she said after her boyfriend died, some men in the group came on to her strong. Their women didn't like that. As they were traveling north, on the outskirts of Live Oaks, the women pushed her and the children out of the van and sped off."

"Good night!"

Lucy shook her head. "I wonder where she got the virus."

"There's no telling."

"Esmeralda, I know being a hooker is a bad sin, but what else could Maria do? I can see why she wound up like she did—couldn't speak the language, had no way to feed her children. Afraid of the law . . ."

"It's sad, Lucy, it's sad. And to think such as that went on right under our noses."

I could see Thelma was still in there with Maria, and I knew she would stay long enough for me to get my ducks in a row. Lucy was talking a mile a minute.

"I know. I see stuff like that on TV, but it's hard to believe it's happened right here in Live Oaks. Maria wanted to tell me more, but she was given out. Maybe I can get some more out of her later." Lucy brushed a strand of hair out of her face. "What did you find out at the courthouse?"

I started toward the kitchen to get busy on the phone. "Can I tell you about it later?" I asked. "I need to make some phone calls."

"Sure. Oh, by the way, Beatrice called. She said to tell you she and Carl went to church and that Carl is bald on top and uses his pigtail to do a comb over. She fixed Sunday dinner for him, and the couple upstairs also ate with them."

I couldn't help but smile at that. "Thanks, Lucy, I'll try to call her. But right now I have got to find us a lawyer."

Lucy put her hand on my arm. "One more thing," she said, looking worried. "Maria's afraid to die."

Well, that piece of information didn't surprise me one bit. I had worried that neither the pastor nor I could speak to Maria about the Lord. "Lucy, since you're the only one speaks Spanish, it's up to you to show her the way."

"Well, I tried to say something."

"Good . . ." I walked over to the window; somebody was pulling up in the driveway. It was the cruiser, with Horace at the wheel. *I wonder what he wants?* I walked out to the porch to meet him.

Well, Horace wasn't nearly the officer of the law chasing me on the highway; he looked like a shorn sheep, drooped shoulders, head down. He got out of his car and walked over to me.

"What can I do for you, Horace?"

"Miss Esmeralda," he said softly, "you said I should come and see for myself."

"You want to see Maria?"

"Yes'm." He fingered the cap he held in his hands, looking scared to death.

"Well, all right," I said. "I'll see if you can."

Well, it wasn't all right. I went into the sickroom to have a peek and found that Maria had started coughing and was spitting up blood. I turned around and started to tell Horace to wait a minute, but I didn't. I figured he might as well see what it was like to have AIDS.

I beckoned to him, and he followed me in. After not a minute, that poor boy was gagging on the odor of the sickroom. He bolted out of there. I could hear retching, gagging, and some more throwing up.

"What's the matter with Horace?" Thelma asked. She was helping Lucy clean up Maria.

"He's sick to his stomach. Listen, girls, I've got to try to find us a lawyer, and if I don't call now, their offices will be closed."

"Go ahead, we can manage," Thelma said.

Being a law-abiding citizen, I was not personally acquainted with a single lawyer in the county, and with the reputations lawyers have got, I wondered if I could find a good one who wouldn't squeeze the last penny out of us. I was thumbing through the yellow pages and, wouldn't you know it, here came Horace back inside.

"I'm sorry, Miss Esmeralda. I got to clean up that mess out here on your front porch."

"The front porch! Mercy me, boy, couldn't you make it to the yard?" I wet a washcloth and handed it to him, then went to the broom closet to get the stuff he needed to clean the porch. I gave him detergent, a bucket, my scrub broom, and a can of disinfectant. "Use the garden hose in front to wash it off. Be sure you scrub the porch and spray it good with disinfectant. Try not to leave any sign or smell of that vomit on my porch."

I didn't mean to sound harsh, but I know I did. When I had a minute, I'd apologize or make it up to him some way. That poor boy was going through hell with nobody to confide in and no mother to comfort him.

I went back to the yellow pages, where there were names and ads of lawyers all over the county, as well as from Columbia. I couldn't count the number of those full-page ads of accident attorneys. What we had to deal with was no accident.

I scanned page after page but got nowhere.

Horace finally shut off the hose and gathered up the cleaning stuff to bring back inside. He walked around the house and came in the back door.

"Horace, look in the fridge and get yourself some ginger ale. That'll help settle your stomach."

The boy looked so pale and scared, I really felt sorry for him. "You'll have to look for it—it's way in back somewhere."

After poking around and making me nervous, he finally found the ginger ale and stood in the middle of the floor, not knowing where to find a glass.

"Go in the laundry room, Horace. You'll find a paper cup in that package on the washer."

He found it, poured himself the cold drink, and sat across from me at my kitchen table. "Thanks," he said.

I grunted and turned the page.

"What're you looking for?"

That was none of his business, so I didn't answer. The boy just wanted to talk, and I was too busy to talk right then.

"I got tested today."

I looked up from the phone book. "At the hospital?"

"No, the med center."

Well, I knew why he didn't go to Carson City General—it was too close to Live Oaks and he didn't want his business spread all over the county.

"They say it'll take seven to ten days before I'll know anything."

Watching me turn another page and run my finger down the list of names, he asked again, "What're you looking for?"

Ordinarily, I would have told him it was none of his business, but that poor boy needed what kindness I could give him. "Well, Horace, I'm looking for a good lawyer."

"A good lawyer? Daddy knows all the lawyers in the county and in Columbia too. If you need a lawyer, he's the one to ask."

I was in no position to ask Sheriff Thigpen for any favors, but I wasn't getting anywhere searching the yellow pages. Lucy was calling me.

"All right, Horace, ask your daddy to give me a call. And today, Horace. Right away."

Sure enough, as soon as Horace got home and told him, Thigpen called me. I gave him all the details, and he said he'd get right on it.

17

Lucy and I were giving Maria her morning bath when I heard an engine roaring up outside.

"Sounds like a motorcycle," Lucy said.

It was. When I made it to the door, I saw the thing parked in the driveway. A man who looked like one of those long-haired, tattooed bikers was waiting for me.

"Can I do something for you?" I asked.

"Esmeralda! Don't you recognize me?"

With that helmet and goggles, he didn't look like anybody I'd have the least interest in knowing. He pulled off the helmet and goggles and laid them on the glider, then unzipped his leather jacket. Well, I tell you, if I had a belly like his, I would never unzip my jacket.

"No, I don't know you, and we've got sickness here. Get to the point, mister. State your business."

"Esmeralda, it's Percy Poteat!"

"Percy Poteat?" He looked worse than roadkill. "What funny farm did you escape from?"

"Ha! Aren't you going to invite me in?"

Invite him in and it's inviting trouble, more of which I don't need, I thought. "Well," I said, hesitating, "you can come in, but I can't give you more than a few minutes. Like I said, we have got sickness here."

He opened the screen door.

"Wipe your feet, Percy," I ordered, pointing to the rug. I tell you, I didn't like this one bit. Nothing good could bring Percy Poteat back to Live Oaks after all these years. Why, he hadn't even come back for his own mama's funeral!

"Esmeralda, how about a drink?"

"A drink of what?"

"I know you don't have tequila, so I'll settle for anything you got."

"You'll settle for ice tea, because that's what I've got."

He followed me into the kitchen and sat down at the table. As I poured the tea, I asked him, "Where's your eyeglasses?"

"Oh, I wear contacts now."

"Well, then, what brings you to Live Oaks?"

"I'm looking for me a wife."

He didn't sound one bit embarrassed about that.

"I hear you've had half a dozen or more."

"Ha! Not that many, but close." He lifted the cake lid and helped himself to a slice of Clara's pound cake. "Esmeralda, I've made some bad choices," he said as he touched a big gold cross that hung on his chest, along with a bunch of other gold chains. "But I've turned my life around. I'm on the right road now, and it brought me straight home to Live Oaks. I'm looking for the one I should've married in the first place."

"And who might that be?"

"Why, Esmeralda, don't you remember how crazy Beetriss was about me?"

I folded my arms across my chest. "Percy, just what are you getting at?"

"She's not married, is she?"

"Percy, by her own choice, Beatrice is not married. And you're wasting your time if you think she would give you the time of day."

Actually, I wasn't sure that was the case, but I felt it was my duty to nip this thing in the bud. Just when Beatrice had started enjoying Carl's company, here this creep shows up.

Percy helped himself to another piece of cake. "Before she died, Mama wrote me what a good cook Beetriss was. None of my women could cook worth a toot." He talked with his mouth full as he wolfed down the cake. "Beetriss got any property? I guess she owns her own home, right?"

I gave him a look that would have wilted an artificial cornflower. "What Beatrice owns or don't own is none of your business."

"Ha! Same old Esmeralda—feisty as the devil." With elbows on the table, he leaned forward. "Esmeralda, what Beetriss needs is me. I can give her what she's never had—excitement. Once she learns to handle a Harley, we could travel the country. See that Grand Canyon she's always wanted to see."

I was surprised he remembered that about Beatrice. But I didn't show it. "You are whacko if you think Beatrice would ever straddle a motorcycle and tear around the country like some wild, crazy female."

Percy shrugged. "She won't know until she tries it. There's nothing like it in the world. These babies can go a hunnert miles an hour, just cruising. She'll love it."

I'll be honest with you—you just can't tell about women me and Beatrice's age. We do foolish things sometimes, get roped in by con artists and the like. I thought that with all the sense Beatrice had not got, she might think Percy Poteat was an answer to prayer—believe that cock-and-bull story about turning his life around, get goose pimples over him, or think she could keep him from trying to kill himself on the highway.

"Where's she living now?" he asked.

"She doesn't live here anymore."

"Where'd she move to?"

"Up the road."

A cake crumb escaped onto Percy's chin. "You wouldn't be trying to discourage a fellow, would you?"

"Percy, I can't fool with you any longer. Like I told you, there's a sick woman here."

"You got Beetriss's number?"

"I do, but I don't have time to look it up."

He got my drift; he wasn't going to get any more information out of me. And he didn't like it one bit.

"I can find her without your help, Esmeralda. All I got to do is ask at Apostolic Church—the preacher'll give me her address."

He left in a huff, banging the door behind him.

He was right. It wouldn't be hard for him to find Beatrice. But I'd done my best. The Lord would just have to look after her from here on out.

As I watched Percy roar out the driveway, the phone rang. Sheriff Thigpen was on the line. "Esmeralda, I found the man you're looking for. He's the best lawyer Columbia's got—Seth Tobias. He's going to run for congress next year, so he's anxious to help you out. He said if those children were born in the States, then they're American citizens. All you have to do is get their mother to sign over the adoption papers. Seth says you can just turn it all over to him, and he'll handle everything."

What a relief! Thank the Lord. Hallelujah! "Sheriff, I don't know how to thank you. Where do I get them papers?"

"Horace is on his way to Columbia right now to pick them up. Once you get the papers signed, he'll take them back to Seth."

I put down the phone and thanked the Lord. Of course, I knew we had a ways to go yet. Explaining things to Maria and getting her consent to the adoption wouldn't be easy. And if the children's tests came back positive, I couldn't ask the Osbornes to adopt them. But we'd just cross that bridge when we came to it. Right now, we had to work fast. I knew Maria could pass away before we got anything settled.

I heard a truck turning in the driveway; it was Elmer this time. I met him at the back door and helped him bring in the jars of beans, soup mix, and corn the W.W.s had canned for me. Elmer took the jars down in the basement, and I went with him to see they were put on the right shelves.

As he was leaving, he asked if there was anything he could do for me. "Well, Elmer, we made the last payment on a tiller I bought for Elijah, and I wonder if you might have time to bring it up here in your truck? I bought it from a woman who lives on the corner of Elm and Oak."

"Mrs. Brown lives there—husband died a little while back?"

"Right. There's no hurry, but if it's convenient, I would appreciate it."

"I'll have it up here soon as I can."

After Elmer left, I went back to see about Maria. She was sleeping, and Lucy was straightening up the room.

"Sit down, Lucy," I said. "I've got some good news. Sheriff Thigpen called, and he's got us a lawyer down in Columbia who says he'll handle everything. He's a man by the name of Seth Tobias. I don't know him, but I've seen his name in the paper. He told the sheriff that if the children were born in the States, then they are American citizens and there'll be no problem about adoption. From what you've told me, this seems to be the case. Didn't you get the idea that all three of them were born here?"

"I did. I paid close attention, and I remember she told me that Carlos, the oldest boy, was born in California, and the others along the way through the South to Florida."

"Good. Maria will have to sign a paper to that effect. Do you think you can explain all this to her and get her consent about the adoptions?"

"I think so. I'll try." She paused. "If the Osbornes want to adopt the children, I believe Maria will be glad to sign the papers. When Preacher Bob comes in here and kneels by her bed and holds her hand, she never wants him to leave. She just holds on to his hand as long as she can, and after he leaves, she asks me to tell her about Jesus."

I shook my head. "There's just one drawback, Lucy. We can't say anything to the Osbornes before we get the tests back on the children."

Lucy remembered something. "Oh, I forgot. Dr. Elsie called. She said she'd get back in touch with you."

My heart beat faster. "I'll go call her now."

On my way out of the room, Lucy asked, "Oh, by the way, who was that guy on the motorcycle?"

"Well, all I can say is, he is a creep from way back!"

18

Later in the week, while the hospice nurse was checking Maria's medications, Lucy walked down to the mailbox and brought me back a letter from Beatrice. I was anxious to know if Percy had tracked her down, although he'd hardly had the time. Apparently, he hadn't found her. Beatrice asked about Maria and said she was praying for her. Then she apologized for taking my time to tell me about what was going on with her.

Esmeralda, you would not believe what a wonderful Christian man Carl is. His Bible is falling apart and he knows what's in it from cover to cover. He told me there are three hundred and eighty "fear nots" in the Bible and I've been looking them up. You won't believe this, but those verses are helping me not to be so afraid about things.

I've been cooking a lot here lately and when Carl comes I invite Sadie and Jim from upstairs to eat with us. As you know, whatever I eat I might as well rub it on my hips because that is where it's going. I have gained nearly ten pounds. All my clothes are too tight so I had to buy more. Sadie works in an office and is a real stylish dresser, so I asked her if she would go shopping with me one Saturday. While we went shopping Jim and Carl went fishing. I would never have found the cute outfits Sadie found for me. She said with the color of my hair I could wear yellow and green as well as autumn colors.

I tell you, Sadie should have been a beauty parlor operator. When she fixes my hair Carl and Jim both tell me how nice it looks.

Jim and Sadie don't fight like they use to although sometimes I can hear them fussing and sometimes they don't speak to each other for a day or two. But when they're with us, with me and Carl, we all have a good time. Jim is such a cutup, he keeps us laughing. He and Carl watch the Braves games on TV and while they're watching TV, I'm in the kitchen with Sadie teaching her how to cook.

We all went bowling the other night. I'm not very good at it. They're trying to teach me how to throw the ball so it don't roll down along the side. They don't know it, but I'm doing good if I don't go sliding down the

*alley on my backside. I wish they'd just let me keep
score.*

*Esmeralda, I want you to pray for Sadie and Jim.
Carl is talking to them about the Lord but they aren't
interested in going to church with us.*

*I better sign off. I have a cake in the oven. It's
Jim's birthday and we're going to surprise him.*

Well, mercy me, it sounded too good to be true. It
sounded like Beatrice was happier than she'd ever been
in her entire life. I smiled as I folded up the letter. *Now
if that jerk Percy Poteat don't throw a monkey wrench
into the situation, who knows? Maybe Beatrice will wind
up marrying Carl. Wouldn't that be something!*

When the nurse was ready to leave, I walked out on
the porch with her. "What do you think?" I asked.

"She's much weaker. She's asking for the children.
Maybe you ought to bring them over so she can see them
one more time."

"All right, I'll do that. Thanks for all your help."

Before I called Pastor Osborne, I had to get my ducks
in a row. Horace had brought the papers, but Lucy had
not talked with Maria to make certain where the children were born and so forth. I shuffled through the
papers and found three that dealt with citizenship. With
those papers in my hand, I went back in the room.

Maria's eyes were closed. "Lucy, do you think you can
talk to her now? Or is she sleeping?"

"No, I don't think she's sleeping."

"Well, these are the papers she has to sign, saying where each of the children were born."

Lucy took the papers and read one. "Esmeralda, her signature has to be notarized."

"Notarized?" I repeated. Hmmm. That was a problem. I didn't know any notary republic but Elmer, and he was at work. I went back in the other room and looked at the adoption papers. They, too, had to be notarized. I called Elmer and asked him if he could leave work long enough to notarize Maria's signature, and he said to just call him when we were ready.

After I hung up, I realized that we wouldn't be ready with the adoption papers until we'd heard from Dr. Elsie. And she hadn't called back yet.

I picked up the phone and called her office. The girl at the desk said the doctor wasn't in, but that she had left a message for me. "Miss Esmeralda, Dr. Elsie wanted you to know that the children's tests came back negative."

"That means they don't have the virus?"

"That's right."

"All three of them?"

"All three of them!"

I could hardly believe my ears! I ran into the bedroom to tell Lucy. "It's a miracle! It's a miracle, Lucy!"

We hugged each other and cried like babies. I had to get us calmed down, though, because there was so much to do.

"Now, Lucy, I'm going to call the pastor and have him bring over the children. There are all these papers Maria has to sign, and she's so weak we need to get on this right away. Before the children come, maybe you can get her signature on the citizenship papers. Don't worry about them being notarized; when Elmer comes, he'll notarize them along with the other papers."

I looked at Maria and could tell she was sinking fast. "Lucy, we don't have much time. After the children leave, it won't be easy, but you'll have to talk to her about the adoptions."

As excited as I was about the children's report, I was getting nervous that maybe we'd waited too long to take care of all this business. I called the Osbornes, and Betty said the children were playing in the wading pool Mrs. Purdy had ordered for them, but that she'd get them over here as quick as she could.

A little while later, I heard yet another vehicle coming up the driveway. It was Horace this time. I figured he was ready to take the papers back to Columbia and would hang around until they were signed. I slipped back into the sickroom to see if Maria was awake enough to sign the citizenship stuff.

I heard the screen door close, and in a minute or two Horace was at the bedroom door. His voice was trembling when he called my name.

I walked out of the room to greet him, and I couldn't believe what I saw. His face was white as cold ashes, and tears were streaming down his cheeks.

"Horace! What's the matter?"

He turned his back and doubled over crying.

I put my arm around him and led him to the kitchen.

"Close the door," he said, sobbing.

I closed the door and turned back to him. He sat down, his arms folded on the table, and put his head down. And it came to me what this was all about. Horace had no mama; he couldn't tell his daddy. I was the only one in Live Oaks he could tell that his test came back positive.

I put my arms around him and held him close. And I cried too.

Lucy tapped on the kitchen door. "Esmeralda?"

I dabbed at my eyes with my apron, then poked my head out the door. "Yes, Lucy?"

"Don't you think I should put that new gown on Maria that the ladies brought her?"

"Yes, let's do that."

I patted Horace on the shoulder and left the kitchen to go help Lucy put Maria into the pretty gown. It was one of those silky kind with little pink rosebuds around the neck. The W.W.s had made up the money to buy it, and a committee went to get it while it was on sale.

Once we slipped the gown onto that frail body, Lucy touched up Maria's face with some blush and brushed her hair. I handed Lucy Maria's Spanish comb.

"Did you talk to her yet?" I asked as Lucy gently placed the comb in Maria's hair.

"Some. Carlos was born in California, Rios in Texas, and Angelica in Florida. I've filled in the states on their papers, but she's so weak she's having a hard time remembering their birthdays."

"I tell you what to do. The children told you their ages. Carlos is five, Rios is four, and Angelica is three. If Maria can remember the months they were born in, we'll just make up the dates."

Lucy nodded. "I guess we'll have to."

I left Lucy talking to Maria and went back to Horace. His head was still down on the table, but he was not crying as hard. I put two slices of bread in the toaster and poured him a glass of milk. "You had breakfast?"

He didn't answer. I got out the butter and jam. "Would you like some oatmeal?"

He raised his head. "No thanks."

He blew his nose and sat there with his elbows on the table, with his head in his hands, looking down at the placemat.

The toast popped up. I took out two plates and served us both a piece.

But the poor boy made no move to eat. "Esmeralda, you said my sin would find me out. I just didn't know I'd get this death sentence."

I reached out to put my hand on his arm. "I know this is difficult, but try to have some hope. You have the virus, but maybe if they treat it early, you'll postpone the AIDS part."

"I guess, in a way, everybody's got a death sentence."

"No, Horace. Christians don't have a death sentence."

"Oh, I don't mean that way. I mean everybody has got to die sometime."

I buttered my toast, lathered it with Thelma's damson jam, and took a bite before I told him, "There's no place in the Bible tells a Christian to look for death. We are to look for the coming of the Lord."

"Well, sure, but—"

"It's the blessed hope, Horace. We won't all die a natural death. When Jesus comes, we'll be caught up to meet him in the air."

"Yeah, I know. All them TV preachers talk about that." He was toying with the toast and not drinking the milk.

"With all that's happening in the world today, there's every reason to believe that Jesus is coming soon. The important thing is to be ready."

I could hear car doors slamming. "That must be Pastor Osborne. I'm sorry. We can talk about this later, okay?" After he nodded his head, I got up and went to meet the children running up the walk.

19

Betty Osborne came with her husband to bring the children. The pastor was carrying Angelica, but the boys were excited, pushing and shoving each other as boys will do. Bringing the children inside, I got them quiet before we went in the room. When they saw their mother, they were as still as church mice. They couldn't take their eyes off her.

We had raised the head of the hospital bed and propped Maria up with pillows so that she looked more alive than she really was. The fragrance of the dusting powder we'd used had a soft scent like lilacs blooming. With the window open, the air was fresh and cool and had none of that hospital smell. And earlier that day, Lucy had gone to my garden and brought in big blue hydrangea blooms, which she put in my glass ice-tea pitcher and set on the dresser. All in all, we'd done everything we could think of to make this last visit as beautiful as possible.

The boys stood close beside the bed, and Pastor Osborne held Angelica in his arms so her mother could see her. Poor Maria couldn't speak above a whisper, and I think that frightened the boys. They stood very quiet. I heard Maria whisper, "Carlos . . ."

Lucy listened carefully and then told me Maria was telling Carlos not to fight with his brother, to be strong, to be good, and to love Jesus. Seeing the little boy's chin quivering, Pastor Osborne laid his hand on his shoulder and drew him closer. Maria was mouthing the words that in any language could only mean "I love you."

Rios's big, dark eyes didn't leave his mother's face as she spoke softly to him. As he listened, unconsciously fingering the edge of the sheet that covered his mother's bones, he looked confused. I knew his heart was aching.

Lucy wasn't sure she understood all that Maria had told him, but she did hear her say that he was a good boy. "Now she's telling both boys to look after their sister, to hold her hand. . . . I can't make out everything she's saying."

Maria looked over to Lucy and said something. "She wants her comb," Lucy told us and proceeded to take the comb out of Maria's hair and put it in her hand. Maria spoke with her eyes, and Lucy understood what she wanted to do. She took the comb, and with some effort, succeeded in putting it in Angelica's fine hair. Angelica reached out her hand to touch her mother's face. Maria was able to press her lips to the palm of that little hand

and then, as if to seal that soft kiss, she folded the tiny fingers over the palm.

I know we were all fighting back tears, but we managed to keep smiles on our faces.

It was time for the boys to say good-bye, so Pastor Osborne handed Angelica to Betty and lifted Rios, then Carlos, to give their mother a kiss. Somehow I felt those little boys knew it would be their last kiss. They primped up but didn't cry.

The comb fell out of Angelica's hair, and Betty retrieved it. "Tell Maria we'll keep it for Angelica," she said.

Lucy repeated this to Maria, who looked like she might not have another breath in her. But as the Osbornes prepared to leave, Maria became frantic.

Lucy stopped them. "Wait, now, let's see what she wants."

Maria was looking up at the pastor, her eyes pleading, her hands trying to grasp his arm.

Pastor Osborne turned to Lucy. "Does she want us to stay?"

Lucy spoke to Maria in Spanish and leaned down close to hear her whisper. "No, Pastor. That's not it. She wants to give her children to you."

Pastor Osborne clasped Maria's hand in his. "Oh, thank her, Lucy. Thank her! Tell her we will love them and care for them and do everything we can to bring them up as she would want us to."

Lucy repeated to Maria what he'd said, but Maria still seemed frantic. She was trying to say something.

Lucy bent down again to hear, then turned to the pastor and his wife. "Maria wants you to adopt the children so they can never be sent back to Guatemala."

"We will," Betty said. "Oh, tell her we will."

Lucy relayed the message. Hearing that, Maria sank back on the pillow and closed her eyes.

"It's time we go," Betty whispered, and they moved toward the door.

I followed them. "Pastor, can you and Betty give me a minute here, please?"

I quickly walked to the kitchen. Horace was still there, and I asked him to take the children to the car while I spoke with the Osbornes.

"Pastor," I said when we were alone, "are you and Betty sure you want to adopt these children?"

As she wiped her tears, Betty answered, "Esmeralda, God himself sent us these darling little ones. They're the answer to our prayers."

They didn't even ask me if the children's tests had come back negative or anything at all about their background. "Okay," I said. "If you're sure this is the Lord's will for you, we need to get the papers signed and your signatures notarized."

It was time to call Elmer.

By lunchtime, all the papers were signed and notarized. Although I wasn't sure anybody could make out Maria's pitiful scrawl, I gave the papers to Horace to take to the lawyer.

When I got back in the room, Lucy was putting a cold cloth on Maria's forehead. I stood looking down at her. "She's slipping away now," I whispered.

Lucy seemed nervous. "Since the Osbornes left, she hasn't opened her eyes. She's hardly breathing at all."

"She's let go, Lucy."

We both sat down. There was nothing to do now but wait.

I was sitting down, but my mind wasn't. It kept racing from one thing to another. But mainly I was thinking about the Osbornes. With the pastor's salary, it was nip and tuck for just him and Betty. With three little ones to feed and clothe, it was going to stretch them beyond their limit.

Of course, as far as food went, I had enough vegetables canned and frozen to feed them all winter, and more besides. And the W.W.s could go through their linen closets and find enough sheets and towels to furnish them. There wasn't a member of the class who didn't have more of that stuff than they ever used. . . . The Osbornes would need a bed or two, and there was plenty of furniture in attics to take care of that. . . . Dr. Elsie could doctor them for free. . . . But even with all our help, the Osbornes would need more money than they were getting now. . . . That little two-door car they had would have to be traded for something bigger.

Suddenly I realized I was getting way ahead of myself. The good Lord would see to it that they were taken care of—the good Lord and the Willing Workers. I knew that once the W.W.s saw what the Osbornes were up against, they'd persuade the deacons to recommend a raise.

Thinking that through, I began to wind down. Drifting in the window was the sound of Boris's lawn mower as he cut Mrs. Purdy's grass. He'd sent word that the young people wanted to help me with whatever housekeeping I needed done. *Maybe tomorrow I'll let them vacuum and dust.*

From time to time, I stood up to take a look at Maria and to stretch my legs. We no longer tried to turn her over or do anything that might disturb her.

As the afternoon wore on, my mind drifted. *No doubt Percy has found Beatrice by now,* I thought. So I prayed for her.

I thought about poor Horace, and I prayed for him too. When his daddy found out, there'd be the devil to pay!

At suppertime Lucy went in the kitchen and made us sandwiches and ice tea. We took turns going to the table to eat.

We'd just finished eating when Dr. Elsie slipped in. She examined Maria, shined a small flashlight in her eyes, held the stethoscope to her neck, looked at her fingernails, and then removed the IV from her arm.

Finally, she looked at Lucy and me. "A few more hours," she said.

Lucy looked scared. "Won't you sit down, Dr. Elsie? Can I get you anything?" She pulled up another chair.

Dr. Elsie took a seat. "Lucy, were you able to lead Maria to the Lord?" she asked in that blunt way she has.

Lucy frowned. "I'm not sure, Dr. Elsie. She seemed hungry to hear about Jesus, and I told her all I knew."

"Did you draw in the net?"

"Draw in the net?"

I tried to explain. "Lucy, Dr. Elsie means, did Maria receive Christ as her own Lord and Savior?"

"Well, Maria couldn't talk much. She never said those words—those words about receiving Christ as her personal Savior. But she cried once, and when I asked her why she was crying, she said she had sinned so bad she couldn't do anything but cry. She was so afraid to die."

Dr. Elsie twisted around in her chair and bore down on Lucy. "Did you explain the way of salvation to her?"

"I'm not sure. I probably didn't say everything I should have said. I told her Jesus loves her and would forgive her if she asked him to."

"Did you tell her Jesus died for her sins?"

I squirmed in my seat. Dr. Elsie was even making me uncomfortable.

"Yes, I told her that more than once."

"But you don't know if she asked the Lord to forgive her?"

"Oh yes. She asked the Lord to forgive her. She asked him out loud, and I heard it. . . . Now that I think about it, she didn't seem so worried after that, and when we talked, it was about the things Jesus did and said."

Dr. Elsie's face softened and she smiled. "Lucy, you drew in the net."

20

Lucy and I thought Maria might last another day, but in the wee hours, at 2:20 in the morning, we could see she wasn't breathing. We both tried to find a pulse, but there wasn't one. The set of her face told me she was dead.

"She's gone," I whispered.

Lucy was trembling.

I pulled the sheet up over Maria, but I didn't cover her face. Somehow I couldn't bring myself to do that. I don't know why.

"She's gone," I repeated. "I'll call Dr. Elsie."

Our conversation was brief. She said she'd come right over.

When I came back in the room, Lucy was pale and so nervous her whole body was shaking.

"Have you never seen anyone die?"

She shook her head.

I thought then of the way Bud died—not peaceful at all. "Well, let's just sit down here and wait for the doctor," I said.

We were quiet for a long time, hearing only the crickets chirping outside. Finally Lucy asked me if we shouldn't call the preacher.

"No," I said, "not at this hour of the morning. There's nothing he can do."

When I heard Dr. Elsie ease up in the driveway, I went to meet her at the door. We greeted each other, but Dr. Elsie was all business; that's the way she is about anything medical. Lucy stood up when she came in the room, but Dr. Elsie went straight to Maria, set down her bag, and began the examination. In just a few minutes, she asked, "What time did she expire?" When I told her, she said, "Esmeralda, I'll see that you get copies of the death certificate by ten o'clock."

Her work done, she turned and looked at Lucy. She probably noticed how nervous the poor girl was, so she sat down and patted the chair next to her. Lucy took a seat. "You two have certainly taken good care of Maria. As soon as you can, you must try to get some rest. It'll be hectic the next couple of days. . . . I've been meaning to say, Lucy, that you can't keep on being the only Spanish-speaking person in Live Oaks. You'll need help in that department. What are we going to do about that?"

"Well, Preacher Bob asked if I had a Spanish dictionary he could use. When there's time, I could teach him and Betty to speak the language. Some of my students can help too."

"Lucy, those children can learn English easier than grown-ups can learn a foreign language. Let's also see what we can do about teaching the children English."

The conversation had calmed Lucy, so Dr. Elsie got up to leave. I went to the door with her, thanked her for coming, and returned to the task at hand.

I asked Lucy if she felt like helping me. She said she did. I could've spared her the unpleasantness, but the sooner a Christian learns about death, the better. It's the devil's masterpiece, death is, and until you have hands-on experience with his handiwork, you don't know what an enemy he is. He is not satisfied that he and Adam brought death into the world. He does his best to drag out the suffering, make death as gruesome and painful as he can.

I pulled the sheet off Maria, balled it up, and tossed it on the floor.

By four o'clock, Lucy and I had finished the work of cleaning up the body and the bed, and I called the undertaker, Boyd Jones. Jones Funeral Home is the only one in town, and when Bud died, they charged me a fortune. I was not going to let that happen again.

Jones came within half an hour. After he rolled Maria out of the house, I told Lucy to go take a hot shower and lie down until breakfast was ready.

For the first time in days, I was hungry.

I got the coffee going, put on the pot for grits and a pan for bacon, set the table, and poured orange juice. By then I could hear Lucy's shower going.

As the bacon was sizzling and the grits were bubbling, I enjoyed the peace and quiet I knew wouldn't last long—as soon as the word spread, a lot of people would be coming and going in the house.

I put the bacon to crisp on paper towels, then stuck some bread in the toaster and scrambled the eggs.

When everything was ready, I fixed our plates and called Lucy. She didn't answer, so I went to the bedroom to see if she was coming. She was out like a light. I smiled and closed the door. *Poor baby. She's plum worn out.*

I ate my breakfast and then went out on the porch to watch the sunrise. The faint rose color was barely inching its way above the town dump. I was feeling good about the way the Lord had worked everything out—the red tape and all. And to think, now the Osbornes had not one but three children.

With daylight coming on, I went back in the house and called Pastor Osborne. He wanted to know when Maria died, all the like of that, and he asked me what he could do to help. There were a few things. I asked him to send someone to tell Elijah that Maria had died.

"Okay," he said. "And I'll ask Betty to pass the word to the W.W.s. Esmeralda, I'll need Lucy here when I talk to the children. Do you think that can be arranged?"

"Oh, sure. She's sleeping right now, but when she wakes up, I'll tell her."

"Good. Now when can I get with you to talk about the service?"

"Pastor, you can just take care of that. Whatever the Lord gives you to say. . . . But there's one thing you can do for me. Write up a little something for the *Journal*'s obituary column."

He said he would.

When we hung up, I knew it wouldn't be long before the house was swarming with people. I had promised Beatrice I would call her when Maria died, so I dialed her number.

She didn't ask a lot of questions, but I went through the details anyway. She wanted to know when the service would be and if she should send flowers. Of course, I didn't know about the service, and I told her she could do what she wanted about sending flowers. As for myself, I like flowers at a funeral. I'm never stingy when it comes to sending flowers.

Beatrice was quiet for a minute, and I was about to hang up when she said, "Esmeralda, guess who's here?"

I heaved a big sigh so she would hear it. "Not Percy Poteat, I hope."

"Yes, it's Percy. He came on his bike."

"Well, I hope he's on his way to some other place by now."

"No, he's still here. He's staying with Sadie and Jim because he said he wants to be near me. He comes down here for breakfast and supper. For lunch I leave sandwiches in the fridge."

"Beatrice, don't have nothing to do with that man. He is just looking for somebody to take advantage of."

"Esmeralda, he looks awful."

"You don't have to tell me. I saw him. He came here to my house a week ago."

"He said you were rude to him."

"Beatrice, rude is too good for Percy Poteat!"

"But, Esmeralda, can't you see he needs help?"

"Beatrice, this is not the time nor the place for me to be discussing that good-for-nothing, low-down, no 'count, rotten, trashy, common creep. This is a house of mourning."

"I'm sorry, Esmeralda. It's just that I want to help him if I can. . . . You don't like him, do you?"

I heaved another sigh. "All right, Beatrice. I'll tell you what I'll do. You hold off on saying or doing anything that will involve you with that creep, and after things settle down here, I'll hop a bus and come up there."

"Would you?" she said.

"I said I would, didn't I? In the meantime, try to get rid of him."

I don't think I have ever been so mad at anybody in my life as I was with Percy Poteat. I was sure the first thing he'd do would be to turn her against Carl and cut off the competition.

Still stewing about him, I got busy straightening up the house. It wouldn't do for a bunch of women to come in here and see it looking like a disaster area. I got out the vacuum and was about to plug it in when the Apostolic van pulled up in the driveway. There must've been twenty young people piled out and come in the door, ready to go to work.

The vacuum woke up Lucy. I hated that it did, but if the pastor was going to break the news to the children, she would have to be there.

"Lucy," I said as she emerged from the bedroom, rubbing her eyes, "I'm putting your breakfast in the microwave. After you eat, you go on to Osbornes' and help the pastor break the news to the children. Then you can get home and to bed. You look pooped."

Lucy nodded sleepily and sat down at the table for breakfast. I heated up her plate and then pitched in to help with the cleaning.

By the time the W.W.s arrived with more casseroles, the house was looking pretty decent. We hadn't done anything in Maria's room, so I turned Thelma loose in there. She got on the phone right away and called the people to come get the hospital bed and the other sickroom equipment we had rented. I unloaded the washer and was about to take the sheets outside to hang on the line when Clara said she'd do it for me. And Mabel Elmwood had sent her maid along with the W.W.s, so they put her to cleaning out the refrigerator.

With so many hands to take care of things, there was nothing left for me to do except answer questions and tell them where things were, so I decided to take a quick bath and change my clothes.

I was pulling up my panty hose when a girl knocked on the door and said somebody wanted to see me.

The funeral director, Boyd Jones, looking like warmed-over death himself, had come with a white spray for the front door—artificial flowers that could've stood a washing. He wanted a dress for Maria. I gave him the pink gown, which somebody had washed and ironed. In his hushed funeral voice, he sounded like a recorded message offering sympathy. Then he asked when I would come down and pick out the casket. I told him I did not rightly know, since I was very busy.

That didn't set well. "As you know, we have those accident victims from the train wreck, so if you don't mind—"

"Mr. Jones, if you don't have time to funeralize my friend, let it be known here and now that there's other funeral parlors in this county we can hire."

"Oh, I'll be glad to funeralize this lady. Come anytime you want and pick out the casket. We have quite a selection."

I thought he was done then, but he didn't leave; he stood there with his hand on the doorknob. As if it were an afterthought, he said, "I understand this lady has no family. As much as I would like to handle charity cases, I can't. The funeral business is my only means of income, and we do well if we have one funeral a month in Live Oaks. I have to ask you, who's going to pay this bill?"

His greedy little eyes looked over his glasses, waiting expectantly. I was in no mood to be nice. "Aren't you jumping the gun, Mr. Jones?"

"Oh, forgive me. You're upset and I understand." He was fishing in his breast pocket for a paper. "If you'll just sign this paper for me, I'll be on my way."

"Mr. Jones, I am not signing no paper! When we come to pick out a casket, I will come in your office and go over the charges. If what you charge is in my price range, you'll get the business. If not, we'll pay you for what services you have rendered, but we'll make other arrangements."

I all but pushed him out the door and closed it behind him. When he was about halfway to his car, he turned around, came back to the door, and knocked.

"Yes?"

"Miss Esmeralda, there will be a viewing tomorrow night."

"No, there won't be. Didn't I tell you that we'll come to your office, and after that we'll decide about the arrangements? Besides, this will be a closed-casket funeral. There will be no gawking at this poor corpse, with people lying about how good she looks."

Of course, after he left, I realized I had made all these decisions on my own. The more I thought about it, the more I knew it would be a good idea to ask the W.W.s to go with me when I went to the funeral home. I told Clara how that man had scalped me when Bud died, and she had a story or two to add to the case.

So she passed the word to all the ladies in the house and called up those who weren't there. She told me that every single one of the W.W.s would go—that they would be ready whenever I was.

Horace Thigpen parked the cruiser on the street and was coming up the driveway when Elmer's truck turned in. Together the two of them lifted out the tiller and took it to the shed in back. Elmer, seeing the house full of people, left without coming inside, but Horace came in the back door.

"Esmeralda, you got a nice tiller there," he said, taking off his hat. "What're you going to do with it?"

"I bought it for Elijah," I said. "I'm keeping it here until we find a way for him to haul it around town."

"I see," he said. "Do you mind if I hang around a while?"

"No. Everybody else is. Looks like the whole town of Live Oaks is here."

He twisted his hat in his hands. "Ain't there something I can do? I just need to be around people right now."

He was one whipped puppy.

"How's your sleeping?" I asked.

He shook his head. "It's off and on."

"Does Dr. Elsie know?"

"Not yet."

"You need to tell her, Horace."

"I know."

"Come on. I'll fix you something to eat."

There were three kinds of potato salad, macaroni and cheese, fried chicken, okra and tomatoes—no end to the stuff people had brought. I wasn't hungry, but I figured it might encourage him to eat if I fixed me a plate.

At first he just nibbled, sipped his drink, and said I made good ice tea. I got him to talking about other things, and little by little he cleaned his plate.

After lunch I asked Clara to tell the women I was on my way to the funeral home and that they could meet me there. Thelma rode with me, and the others came in their cars. We all got there about the same time and piled out to gather in the parking lot. Boyd Jones looked out the door at us and his mouth dropped open. You'd think the Russians were coming!

With Jones in the lead, we trooped into the casket room and stayed in a group, examining all the big ones he wanted us to see. Mercy me, those fancy ones were decked out with chrome enough for a fifties Cadillac.

Boyd Jones wore gloves to impress us with how grand they were and opened the lids so carefully you'd think royalty lay inside.

After we all had a good look at everything displayed, we huddled and made a unanimous decision. Not one of them was what we wanted, so we headed for the door.

Seeing we were leaving, Jones got very excited. "Wait!" he yelled. "I got something in the back room you may be interested in."

We trooped to the back room, where smaller, wooden caskets were lined up in a row. "These are the models we use when there's a cremation."

Well, they looked fine to me. I checked the prices and saw they were much less expensive. I looked around at the ladies, and without exception they approved of the model I liked.

"We'll take this one," I said, pointing to the casket that had the nicest grain to it. "That is, if your other charges are agreeable."

We followed Boyd Jones into his office, and he scrounged up enough chairs for all of us to sit around his desk. He punched his calculator and read out prices. Beads of perspiration wet his forehead, and it was not a hot day. Thelma knew just what to say to get him to change his figures and bring them down to a reasonable price. We must've spent an hour in there, telling him what we would pay and what we would not pay. Before I signed the papers, I made eye contact with each W.W. to make sure I had the support of every one of them.

I must say, we left that man dripping with sweat. But as we came out of that place, we were smiling.

I put the key in the ignition. "Thelma," I said, "Boyd Jones is one crook we have got the best of. Splurgeon had men like him in mind when he said, 'A white glove often hides a dirty hand.'"

By late afternoon, Pastor Osborne came to the house. He showed me the bulletin to make sure it was okay. "I figured we wouldn't have a viewing, right?"

I nodded and read on. The service would be at eleven o'clock the next morning. The Apostolic deacons were listed as pallbearers.

Pastor Osborne said he and Lucy had talked to the children about their mother going to heaven and that Carlos had seemed to be upset. "Lucy said he was asking for Elijah, so we took him down there. Elijah held him on his lap, petted him, gave him a buckeye to put in his pocket. After a while Carlos slipped off Elijah's lap, took him by the hand, and led him down to the creek. They watched the minnows darting in the water and tried to catch one. Before long, he was okay."

After Pastor Osborne left, I was plum dizzy with so many people coming in and going out, cars parked up and down the street. I went in my room and closed the door.

I didn't wake up until the next morning.

21

It was such a sweet service. The church was full when I arrived with Betty, Lucy, Elijah, and the children in my car. (Me and the W.W.s had saved money by cutting out the limo service Boyd Jones had insisted was necessary for a first-class funeral.) Those three little ones were dressed in new outfits and new shoes, and Angelica's hair was curled in ringlets framing her precious face.

As we stood waiting in the vestibule, I noticed that the ceiling fan was stirring the air and all the windows were open. But with so many people packed in there, it was still humid. Angelica, sucking her thumb, was clinging to Betty's skirt, so Betty picked her up and held her.

Clara's granddaughter was up front in the church playing something sad on her violin. When she finished, Mabel did her best to get something going on the organ, but it didn't sound like the organ was cooperating. Mabel never took organ lessons, and playing by ear don't always work good.

Elmer ushered Betty, the children, Lucy, Elijah, and me to our pew up front. Then Boyd Jones, dressed in a swallowtail coat, ruffled shirt, and string tie, escorted the deacons in, and they filed into the front pew on the other side. Soon the pastor came down the aisle, carrying the cross and calling out the words, "I am the resurrection and the life."

Those words always stir my soul; that day, they made me so glad, I felt like shouting.

Boyd was too cheap to hire an assistant to help bring in the casket. Or maybe an assistant was one of the corners Thelma had cut when we were haggling with the man. Anyway, Boris helped him bring in the casket and arrange the spray on top.

The spray of pink roses was from the W.W.s, and Beatrice's basket of gladiolus was at one end of the casket. At the other end was a big bunch of my hydrangeas some of the women had arranged. There were other arrangements too—mostly from whatever was blooming in backyards and on fences. I had ordered four red roses, and they were in a florist vase setting on the piano. Roses are not cheap. I had arranged with Boris to use them in the service as a nice final touch.

Pastor Osborne opened the service with a short prayer thanking the Lord for making it possible for people in Live Oaks to go to heaven. Then he had us sing "Amazing Grace." Nowadays you don't have to be a Christian to know the song by heart. People in Apostolic Bible love to harmonize on that one, and poor Mabel got so confused she couldn't keep up. In the middle of the third verse she quit trying.

Pastor Osborne never gives us one of those mail-order funerals—the cut-and-dried kind that preachers read out of a black book. For Maria's service he read the words of Jesus: "Take heed that ye despise not one of these little ones; for I say unto you that in heaven their angels do always behold the face of my Father, who is in heaven."

He closed the Bible and talked about Maria's devotion to her children, how she did everything she could to care for Carlos, Rios, and Angelica. Then he paused, looked down at Elijah sitting with the boys on either side of him, and smiled. "When this little family was living in a box-car, the Lord used his servant Elijah. When Maria and the children needed food, he went to the store for them. Since Maude died, Elijah has had to walk everywhere he goes, so a trip to the store meant walking to and from town.

"But I reckon the most important help he gave was watching over the children when Maria couldn't. And when she got so sick it looked like she might die, Elijah went for help. It's no wonder that Maria's children are devoted to him. As you can see, Carlos and Rios have bonded with Elijah." Then, speaking directly to Elijah, he said, "Elijah, Betty and I want you to know that you will always be a member of our little family."

The awesome truth in back of Maria's coming to Live Oaks was probably something new for most of the people listening, but I had thought of it many times. Pastor Osborne explained that the Lord, in his providence, had brought Maria and the children to Live Oaks and to the Lord's people of Apostolic Bible because he trusted us.

The pastor's face just lit up as he talked on. "What a wonderful thing it is to know that the Lord is trusting us with three of his little lambs. Let us covenant together—those of us who are officers and workers in this church, grandparents, parents, and young people—to live holy lives before these children, that they might see Jesus in us and come to love him as we do.

"We are not perfect people, but gross sin in my life or yours can keep a child from coming to the Lord. Jesus said, 'It is impossible but that offenses will come; but woe unto him, through whom they come! It were better for him that a millstone were hanged about his neck, and he cast into the sea, than that he should offend one of these little ones.'"

I could hear snifflings in back of us, and I figured that was a good thing. Maybe folks were ashamed of the way they'd been living.

The pastor then read a pretty poem about stepping on-shore and finding it heaven, and I liked hearing him say he was confident that Maria had stepped on that shore, because she was trusting Christ as her Savior from sin. "We were all praying for Maria," he said, "but were frustrated because we didn't speak Spanish and couldn't talk to her about the Lord. But God had gone before as he always does, and Lucy was here to speak her language and tell Maria about Jesus."

Lucy tucked her head and looked down at her hands folded in her lap.

Well, the pastor knows me well enough not to mention my name from the pulpit, and he didn't this time either, although he thanked the W.W.s and all those who had helped to love Maria into the kingdom.

At the close of the service, the hymn was announced, and Mabel tried to get the organ going. When she couldn't, Boris picked up the tune, and we all sang "Blest Be the Tie That Binds." That hymn always makes my heart tender toward all those hard-to-get-along-with brothers and sisters in Christ.

As we sat there waiting for the young people to remove the flowers and take them out to the grave, I could see Mabel Elmwood up there at the organ so mortified her face was all primped up, ready to bust out crying. *I could be a little nicer to her,* I thought.

When everything was in order at the burial site, Elmer ushered us outside. We had only a short distance to walk to the graveyard. The Jones funeral tent was set up out there with chairs enough for us who were serving as the family.

Pastor Osborne stood with his Bible open, waiting until the people had gathered around the tent. Then he began reading, "'Suffer the little children to come unto me, and forbid them not for such is the kingdom of heaven.'" Closing the Bible, he told us, "I'm looking down at the faces of three little children, and their beautiful dark eyes are looking up at me with that innocence all of us had when we were their age. . . . Our innocence was short-lived, wasn't it? Growing older, we sinned in many ways, didn't we? Fortunately, there is a way whereby we can be made innocent again, as innocent as

Carlos, Rios, and Angelica are today. That innocence is a gift. It comes to us when we transfer all our guilt onto Jesus. He takes the judgment, and we are acquitted, declared innocent once again. We stand before God the Father, not in our sins but in the righteousness of Christ."

Then Pastor Osborne reached down and took Angelica in his arms. Holding her, he walked a few steps back and forth, giving everyone an opportunity to see her. Then he quoted more of Jesus' words: "'Except ye be converted and become as little children, ye shall not enter into the kingdom of heaven. . . . Whosoever, therefore, shall humble himself as this little child, the same is greatest in the kingdom of heaven. . . . And whosoever shall receive one such little child in my name receiveth me.'"

Before he put Angelica down, he motioned to the boys to stand up. "Maria's children have learned a song they're going to sing for us."

Lucy placed Angelica between Carlos and Rios, and the boys held their sister's hands. I was afraid they would be too shy to sing, but once Lucy got them started, their sweet little voices began to sing in Spanish "Jesus Loves Me."

Boris removed the roses from the vase.

I reached in my bottomless pit for tissues, pulled out a handful, and handed them to him so he could wrap the stems. He handed one rose to each of the children and helped them lay the roses on their mother's casket. Then Boris gave Carlos the fourth rose. Lucy whispered something to him, and Carlos handed the rose to Betty. Betty hugged and kissed him.

As far as I could tell, there was not a dry eye in the crowd.

22

❦

After the funeral I hardly had time to catch my breath before packing a bag and going to see what I could do for Beatrice. It was hard to believe that she would risk what she had going with Carl to let Percy Poteat bamboozle her. But a man like that knows what a woman like Beatrice wants to hear—"I need you" or some such tommyrot.

Horace offered to drive me to the bus station, so I let him. On the way into town, he was full of talk. "Esmeralda, now that my days are numbered, I have got to get busy doing things for the Lord."

"Well, Horace—"

"That funeral must've cost a bundle. Boris said the Apostolic youth are going to have car washes to help pay, but car washes won't do it. I know lots of people in town who'll shell out for something like this, so I'm going around and collecting as much as I can get. If it ain't enough, I'll ask Elmer to donate a microwave or something else we can raffle off."

"You will do no such thing, Horace. Apostolic people don't beg, and we don't raffle stuff off. The Lord will provide in his own way. If somebody wants to give toward the expenses, they will give without being asked."

The car was headed for the ditch. "Look out!" I yelled.

Horace righted the cruiser and slowed down to a snail's pace. "Esmeralda, I don't understand you church people. You'd be a lot better off if you ran it like a business. There's foundations and grants with plenty of money to give away, but you're too proud to ask for it. Well, it's your church and you can rock along in the same old ruts if you want to. All I want to do is make it up to the Lord for what I've done wrong so when I face him, he'll let me in."

"You can't make it up, Horace."

"Whadda you mean I can't make it up? I don't believe that. I'm desperate, Esmeralda. I'm so desperate I've decided to give my truck to Elijah." He kept slapping the steering wheel again and again. "I love that old Ford, and I wouldn't part with it for love nor money if I wasn't desperate. It ain't that I can't get by without it. I can. If I'm not driving a city vehicle, I'll have the cruiser. It's just that I hate to part with that old truck. It's been setting up on cement blocks in the backyard, but as soon as I get it fixed, I'll see Elijah gets it."

I looked over at his grim face. "That's good, Horace. He'll appreciate it. But don't think for one minute that will take you to heaven."

"Well, I can do more."

We were rolling into the bus station, and I could see my bus had arrived and was ready to pull out. As I climbed out of the cruiser, I told him, "Horace, what you need to do is go see Pastor Osborne. Ask him how to get to heaven."

Horace lifted my bag out of the trunk and set it down beside the bus. The driver ticketed it and stashed it in the baggage compartment. "Wanna check your shopping bag?" he asked. I told him no, I'd take it on board. The shopping bag was full of canned stuff for Beatrice, and I didn't want to risk the jars getting broke.

The driver jumped on the bus and slid under the wheel, ready to go. I put my foot on the step so he couldn't leave me behind. "Now, Horace, you go see Pastor Osborne."

"Okay. I'll do that," he said.

The driver revved up the motor. "Let's go, lady!"

"Just a minute," I said. "Another thing—go see Dr. Elsie."

The bus lurched forward, and I had to step inside quick. The driver shut the door behind me, so I couldn't hear what Horace was saying. Before I could get sat down, that bus swerved around the station and went sailing down the street.

I didn't realize how tired I was until I sat on that bus. I settled back in the seat, knowing I'd fall asleep once we were on the road. What lay ahead was not going to be easy, but as I mulled over the situation I came up with an ace or two up my sleeve.

With that all decided, I slept most of the way to Piney Woods Crossroad, even though the bus stopped ever so often to pick up more passengers. I'd open my eyes to see who was coming on board, but I didn't know any of them. So I'd close my eyes again, and the sound of the singing tires would put me right out in no time flat.

I woke up for good when we slowed down getting into town. With one hand I got a grip on my shopping bag and with the other hand I held on to my bottomless pit. I sat forward in my seat, anxious to see if Carl would bring Beatrice to meet me. *It sure better not be Percy on that motorcycle!* I thought.

The bus rolled into the station, wheezing and spewing fumes enough to pollute the whole town. Making my way down the aisle behind a lot of fat people, I craned my neck trying to spot Beatrice, but I didn't see her.

In fact, when I got off the bus, I didn't see her for a full minute. If she hadn't called my name, I might've missed her because she did not look like the same person. Upon my word, she looked great—some meat on her bones had done wonders, and she was all decked out in a neat little yellow suit with piping trim and a pale yellow blouse. I couldn't believe my eyes!

We hugged, and I saw a young man in back of her who looked like he was waiting to be introduced.

"Esmeralda, this is Jim, the man who lives upstairs."

We shook hands, and he said we could go on to the car, that he'd get my bag for me.

Beatrice and I went to the car to wait, and after I told her how good she looked, I asked her, "I thought Carl might bring you to the station to meet me. Is he working?"

"No, he's not working today."

She went silent on me. I stood it as long as I could. "Why didn't he come?"

She sighed. "Carl hasn't been around the last couple of days."

"I see." Well, I didn't have to ask why. The reason was Percy Poteat. I could see it would take every ace I had got to get this thing straightened out.

Sure enough, when Jim pulled to a stop in front of the apartment, there was Percy's Harley parked under a shade tree, and his fat self was sitting on the porch, eating a banana.

You would've thought I was the Queen of England the way he greeted me. He even tried to give me a hug! But I just brushed right past him. Jim brought in my stuff, and I took the shopping bag to the kitchen to show Beatrice what I had brought her. Wouldn't you know it, Percy followed us into the kitchen like he owned the place.

I turned on him. "Percy, I have come all this distance to see Beatrice, not you. You go upstairs with Jim or go anywhere you like, just leave us be. I intend to visit with Beatrice, and I'd just as soon not see your face."

He laughed. "Esmeralda, you don't mince words, do you? Okay, I'll go upstairs. There's a game on, but I'll be down at suppertime."

I watched him leave the room, then went in the bathroom to freshen up. When I came out, Beatrice had tears in her eyes.

"What's the matter?" I asked.

"Come sit on the couch with me," she said.

I did and waited to hear whatever it was she had to say.

"Esmeralda, it's been a long time since I have heard you talk that way to somebody."

"What do you mean?"

She took a deep breath. "It's the way you use to be before Bud came home from the war. Back then, if anybody crossed you, you were quick to take off their head."

I laughed. "Oh, I did not!"

"Yes, you did. Remember years ago how you hurt Clara's feelings so bad she dropped out of the youth group? You even laughed about it."

I felt my face flushing.

"I was about the only friend you had," Beatrice went on. "People just wouldn't put up with the way you treated them, but that didn't bother you one bit . . ."

"What do you mean?"

"Esmeralda, I don't think you ever realized this, but when Bud started dating you, you were on top of the world. . . . All the girls were jealous that the biggest catch in Live Oaks was sweet on you. Then when you two got married, people used to say it went to your head."

I was shocked at that, but I was doubly shocked that I was hearing this stuff from Beatrice!

"Bud spoiled you, Esmeralda—gave you everything you wanted. You were pretty selfish, remember?"

"Was I?"

Beatrice nodded her head. "You would go shopping and buy everything for yourself and nothing for Bud."

That hurt me to the quick. I guess it hurt so bad because it was the truth. After Bud came back from the war, I realized how selfish I had been. In our early years together we never had a cross word, but I wish Bud had not been so sweet to me. If only he had put a stop to the way I treated him and everybody else, maybe I would have changed. After he came home from the war, I use to cry and try to make him understand I was sorry, but it was too late. There was nothing left of Bud but pain. I know the Lord forgave me, but many a night I cried myself to sleep over it. Finally I had to block it out of my mind.

"I hate to say this, Esmeralda, but you ran over people and you was selfish. But then you changed . . . Bud coming home in such terrible shape, well, I think it melted your heart."

There was a lump in my throat. I didn't want to start crying, so I went in the kitchen and got a drink of water. When I came back, Beatrice was curled up on one end of the couch, and I could see she was not finished with what she wanted to say.

I sat down next to her. "You say I changed?"

"Yes, Esmeralda, you changed. All those years you were taking care of Bud, little by little you changed . . . you changed for the better."

"In what ways did I change?"

"Well, all that suffering made you tenderhearted . . . I mean, you became so mindful of other people . . . you would give the shirt off your back to help anybody. I don't think there is a more unselfish person in Live Oaks than you."

I tell you the truth, I was stunned. This was a very different Beatrice talking to me that way. But I wasn't too surprised not to defend myself about Percy. "Well, Beatrice, I might have been a little sharp with Percy, but—"

"A little sharp? You sounded like the Esmeralda I knew way back then, before you changed—"

"Well, he deserves—"

"Esmeralda, Percy needs Jesus."

"I know, Beatrice, but . . ." I wanted to say she was not the one who should undertake saving his soul, but instead I changed the subject. "What about Carl? You said he hasn't been around the last couple days."

"Carl has put his business up for sale, so he's been busy with buyers."

"Why is he selling?"

"He wants to retire. With the money he gets from the business, he's going to buy himself an RV and travel."

"How do you feel about him?"

"Esmeralda, he's a darling man. He really is. He has helped me so much. I can't begin to tell you. Those 'fear nots' from the Bible have given me such peace about things. . . . I don't hardly get nervous at all now. Carl's not educated or anything, but he knows a lot. When I said something about how my prayers for a cancer cure were not answered, can you guess what he said?"

Well, I couldn't guess at that, not when I could hardly believe my ears. *Cancer* was a word I never thought I would hear come out her mouth.

"Carl said there are many different kinds of cancer, so we can't look for just one big cure to come along and be the end of it. He brought me some newspaper clippings giving information on how research is paying off. Some cancers are being cured. One day I told him about my surgeries, that it's been ten years now. He said that means I'm a survivor."

Beatrice got up and went in the kitchen to see about something. When she came back, she stood at the window with her arms folded, looking back at me. For the first time in my life, Beatrice was in control and I was not. Ordinarily she wouldn't have dared talk to me the way she had. Before, whenever she said anything the slightest bit negative, she would fall all over herself apologizing. But now she stood there, having said all these things about me, and there wasn't the slightest hint that she was sorry. More than that, for once, I didn't have a comeback.

She walked back to the sofa and curled up again. "There's one thing about Carl that drives me up the wall, though. It's that pigtail."

"I thought you said he uses it for a comb over."

"He does, but that's only on Sundays. I have to put up with it the rest of the week."

"Why don't he get himself a rug?"

"I don't know."

I couldn't help but stare at Beatrice. She looked and sounded like a mature woman. If Carl had done all this to make her grow up, he was too important to let go of. "Beatrice, if Carl asked you, would you marry him?"

She didn't hesitate. "He has asked me. Right now everything is on hold. The Lord has brought Percy back into my life, and it's my duty to do whatever I can do for him."

I did not like the sound of that one bit, but there was no use saying anything.

Percy did come down for supper, but so did the couple upstairs. That made it easier for me to be civil to him.

After we finished eating, Jim and Sadie went back upstairs, and Beatrice insisted on my going in the living room to keep Percy company while she cleaned up the kitchen. So I had to sit in there and listen to all that hogwash he was dishing out.

"Boy, that was a good meal," he was saying. "Why, I've eaten in the best restaurants all over this country, and I'm here to tell you, Beatrice has got them all beat."

He propped his feet up on the coffee table and picked his teeth. "I like a shapely woman," he said, "and Beatrice is one shapely woman. At her age she makes forty-year-olds look like slobs. Nice headlights."

Well, I plum boiled over. "For your information, Percy, them headlights, as you call them, are not for real."

His feet came off the coffee table, and he sat up straight. "Whadda you mean?"

"Beatrice has had surgery there—for cancer."

He looked shocked. "You mean . . . ?"

"Both of 'em."

Percy Poteat had nothing more to say. When Beatrice finished in the kitchen and came out in the living room, he stood up, stretched, and said he was going up to bed.

The next morning, before daylight, a noisy motor woke me up. Somebody was cranking a motorcycle. It had to be Percy. I jumped out of bed and looked out the window just in time to see him taking off down the road. I knew in my heart he was gone for good, and I thanked God.

Half an hour later, Beatrice got up and went to work as usual. I don't think she knew Percy was gone, and I didn't tell her. She would find out soon enough. I just hoped and prayed she wouldn't find out that I'd had anything to do with it.

After I read my Bible and prayed, I messed around in the apartment, doing a little housework, rinsing out my panty hose, and going through a couple of magazines. That conversation with Beatrice had left me unsettled. I turned on the TV, but even that did not take my mind off of what was going on.

Before Beatrice came home from work, Carl came to the apartment. I let him in and invited him to wait for her.

He was not a bad-looking man. At least he had an honest face. However, the pigtail poking out beneath his baseball cap was not something any woman would like. He took off his cap, and I could see he was plenty bald on top. As we sat in the living room talking, I wondered why being bald was such a problem for a man like Carl.

He knew all about me, he said. I could've said the same about him, but I didn't. He seemed shy, so I asked him about his work.

"Well, I was in the exterminating business, but I sold it today. That's why I've come over here. I want Beatrice to celebrate with me—go out to eat at the fish camp."

"That's nice," I said. "You two can go out on the town. There's plenty of leftovers for me here."

"Oh no. We'll want you to go with us."

I smiled. "Well, we'll see." I couldn't think of anything more to talk about. I wished Beatrice would hurry up and get home. I settled back in the recliner.

Finally, he ventured, "I got my price for the business—more'n enough to settle my affairs."

"That right?"

"I'm going to ask Beatrice to help me pick out an RV."

"That's nice."

"Maybe not a new one . . . there's a good used one I've looked at . . . not many miles on it."

"I see." For the life of me I couldn't think of anything more to say except that Beatrice ought to be home soon.

"I wish she'd marry me." Right out of the blue, he said it!

"Well, why won't she?"

"I think it's . . . well, I dunno."

Well, I could see plain as day that I had to help this man. "Carl, is there a wig shop in town?"

"Sure, we got a wig shop."

"What would you think of going downtown to that shop and buying yourself a rug?"

He didn't need a minute to think that one over; he was quick to answer. "Esmeralda, I've thought about that a thousand times! But I just can't settle it in my mind that the Lord would be pleased. It seems like it's pure unadulterated pride makes a man get a toupee."

"Well, what's the difference if you do a comb over or if you wear a rug? It's one and the same thing when you come right down to it. We women get perms and use everything we can get our hands on to look our best. There's nothing wrong with wanting to look your best. After all, we are the temples of the Holy Spirit. Carl, I don't want to hurt your feelings, but that pigtail of yours is not a decoration, it's a detraction from whatever good looks God has favored you with."

I thought his eyes were going to pop out of his head. "You mean . . . you mean—"

"I mean it don't look right for a Christian man to go around looking like a leftover hippie."

He sat on the couch, twirling his cap with his finger and looking kind of excited. "Esmeralda, I never thought of it thataway. Tomorrow morning I'm going to the barbershop, and after that I'm going downtown to that wig shop."

I could hear Beatrice at the door fishing for her key. Carl got up to open the door for her, and I tell you the truth, he looked like he could eat her up.

She gave him a worried little smile. "Hello, Carl. Hello, Esmeralda." She laid her pocketbook on the sofa and started for the kitchen. "Esmeralda, you talk to Carl while I get supper ready."

"Beatrice, you're not cooking tonight!" Carl said. "I sold the business today, and we need to celebrate. I want you and Esmeralda to go out to eat with me."

"Oh, that's good. Did you get your price?"

"Yes. And I want you to go with me to pick out an RV."

A funny little frown clouded her face. "Well, you see, it's like this . . ."

I popped out of that recliner. "Carl, will you excuse us a minute? Beatrice, let's go in the kitchen." I led her into the other room and closed the door behind us. "Percy's gone. He left this morning before daylight."

"What do you mean, he's gone? What did you do to—"

"I didn't tell him to leave, if that's what you mean."

"Then why did he go?"

I crossed my arms over my chest. "He left of his own free will."

Well, I was surprised at the way she took it. She just plain looked relieved. "Well, I guess there's nothing left for me to do except pray for him."

The three of us went out to dinner that night, and when we came home, I went to bed and left them sitting in the living room, talking.

Carl didn't leave until midnight. When Beatrice came to bed, she thought I was asleep and shook my shoulder. "Esmeralda, are you asleep?"

"No," I said.

"Esmeralda . . . I'm going to marry Carl."

"Oh? When?"

"As soon as this buyer's loan goes through."

I sat up and gave her a hug. "Oh, Beatrice! I'm so happy for you."

"I am too," she said and laughed a little. "Carl says he'll have money enough to pay all my medical bills, as well as buy the camper. Do you think I should let him pay my bills?"

"I don't see why not. What is money for except to pay bills?" And I laughed.

Beatrice laughed too. "Carl said with what money we have left over and Social Security, we'll be able to travel."

"Well, Beatrice, I can't wait to tell all your friends in Live Oaks! We'll throw you the biggest wedding the town has ever seen!"

"Oh, I dunno. We don't want to spend a lot of money on a wedding."

"You won't have to spend a lot. Just leave everything to me! I don't suppose you've decided where you'll go on your honeymoon?"

"Oh yes. We're going to the Grand Canyon."

On that bus going home, I had a lot to go over in my mind. You might think I would be all caught up in making plans for Beatrice's wedding, but that was not uppermost in my thoughts. The thing I kept turning over and over was that conversation Beatrice had with me when I first got to her apartment. I'd always thought pretty well of myself, but those things she'd reminded me of . . . well, back then, I must've been a real warhorse.

I wasn't so sure I was much different now, though she said I was. Those first things she'd told me had hurt a lot. But I didn't hold it against her. In fact, the Bible says, "Faithful are the wounds of a friend." And the things she said about my changing, well, that was a comfort.

As I rode on that bus going home, I began to understand how the Lord used that cross I'd carried for all those years. I hated to think it took that much suffering to make changes in me, but at least all that pain had not been wasted.

I knew I had a long way to go yet. A long, long way. I hoped I wouldn't ever rest on my laurels and think I had arrived. After all, once a body stops changing, it comes to rest, and you know what that means—you're outta here, six feet under and pushing up daisies.

Margaret A. Graham is the author of seven nonfiction books, one juvenile work of fiction, and two novels, including *Katie*. She conveys her deep love of the Scriptures as a speaker, Bible teacher, and newspaper columnist. Graham resides in Sumter, South Carolina.